HOLIDAY FAKE DATE

GWYN MCNAMEE

CHRISTY ANDERSON

Holiday Fake Date

© 2021 Gwyn McNamee & Christy Anderson

To all the people with crazy families, may your holiday meals be delicious and drama-free.

ACKNOWLEDGMENTS

This is a bittersweet moment because it's time to say good-bye to the Warren family. With Athena's story, we've completed the trilogy of the crazy, meddlesome family we have grown to love so much.

Thank you to Natalie and Renee for being our beta readers on this story and to Stephie and Caoimhe for always providing amazing editing and proofreading. We appreciate your support more than we can ever say.

And finally, thank you to everyone who has spread their love for the Warren Family Holidays Series over the years. We couldn't do it without you.

CHAPTER 1

ATHENA

A long, deep sigh slips from my lips—as one typically does when dealing with Mother—and I roll my eyes for the tenth time since I answered her phone call, even though she can't see me. They're both just natural reactions when the woman who gave me life goes on one of her power trips—which is far too often.

Especially after Artemis and Archimedes basically threw me under the bus with Mother and Father by defying all family rules and marrying who they wanted—for love instead of, and I quote, "a suitable Warren bride"—and left all the expectations of the Warren clan to fall on me.

My days of somewhat flying under the Warren family's ever-so-strict radar are long gone after the last two holidays. Any grace period I had expired after the Warren sons married "poor people." The future of our prestigious name now hangs in the balance, and Mother seems to think the only solution is to ensure I marry someone "appropriate" soon.

In her dreams...

Senior year isn't even over, and the woman already hears wedding bells with some as-yet-unknown suitor. I can smell the set-up a mile away. As soon as her name popped up on the phone, I *knew* this would be about Thanksgiving and she would somehow use my holiday break at home as a match-making endeavor.

And while I'd love to skip what is sure to be another uncomfortable and tension-filled Warren family holiday dinner, I promised Grandmother I'd be there. That's one woman I won't lie to, even if she did give birth to the man helping pull the proverbial strings with Mother.

"Is that a proper response to a question, Athena? A *sigh?*"

I offer another unseen eye roll. "Yes, Mother, to *properly* answer your question...I'll be home for Thanksgiving."

"Wonderful. Do you remember our dear friends, Bill and Kay Clifton?"

"No, Mother. I'm sorry, but I don't."

Lord knows she'd only bring them up if it somehow worked to advance her dream future for me.

"Of course, you do. They used to live here, in the city, before Bill's business took them to Texas for an expansion. Remember you used to play with their son, Cliff, in the pool at the club when you were four years old."

She can't be serious.

"These people named their child Cliff Clifton? Jesus, poor guy. And sorry, but no, I don't remember him at all. Why do you ask?"

Though I'm sure I don't want to know the answer to that question.

"Cliff is in town for the holidays, visiting his grandpar-ents, and I thought it would be an excellent opportunity to invite him over while you're here on break. You have over a week, so you can take him around the city, grab some dinner. You know, so you can catch up."

Oh, no. Oh, HELL no.

Even though I knew it was coming, could *see* it from a mile away, it still feels like a punch in the gut every single time she tries to control my life.

Well, not this time, Mother...

Barely managing to bite back a chuckle, I click on the *SUBMIT* button at the bottom of the form on the Berkeley Student Carpool app, sending my listing LIVE.

Why do I even agree to return to New York anymore?

Perhaps because no matter how shitty Mother and Father treat us based on some ridiculous standards, no matter how stupid their demands might be, deep down, I know it comes from some place of love and concern for our happiness—way deep, deep down. Like subterranean or maybe even Earth's molten core down.

Or maybe I'm a glutton for punishment.

But more than likely, it's because it's expected of me to fall in line, and no matter how hard I might try to fight it, deep down, I'm still a Warren.

Way deep, deep down.

Yet, just because there are expectations doesn't mean I won't do what I can to make Mother's machinations more difficult. Like my little post to the carpool app asking for a ride to New York over break.

Mother drones on and on about Cliff Clifton while I watch for a response to my request like a hawk watching for a mother bird to abandon her young in the nest so it can swoop in and grab a quick meal.

"Mmm, hmm. Okay, sure, Mother."

It doesn't even matter what she said. Any plans she's making will mean nothing if my post is successful.

And almost as if on cue, a notification sounds on my laptop.

Prez272: Can offer you a one-way ride to New York. If agreeable, meet me at Whiskey Jack's at 8:00 pm tonight to discuss finalizing plans.

I pump my fist in the air in silent celebration. Now I can have a bit of an adventure seeing the country, enjoy a little bit of the beautiful fall weather, and decompress before having to deal with the full Warren front and then return for finals. I can see this country in a way that I never could on my own or with the family. An experience any average, ordinary college student would have and just what I need before spending another crazy holiday that's sure to end in tantrums and tears—likely from Mother. Again.

GoddessA: Will see you there. How will I know who you are?

I tap send, and after another few moments of listening to Mother carry on about "how much she's sure Cliff and I have in common," a reply pops up.

Prez272: I have short, wavy brown hair, a beard, and I'll wear a red shirt and a black leather jacket.

This idea seems to get better by the second.

Keys jingle in the lock on the front door, and Valerie, enters, backpack slung over her shoulder.

I wave and point to my phone, rolling my eyes and miming that I'm slowly dying—our sign that I'm on the phone with my parents.

She laughs quietly to herself and heads to the kitchen

island to unload all of her books. It looks like while I'll be making my way across the country with Prez272 slowly enough to miss any exciting dates Mother has planned with poor Cliff Clifton, Valerie plans to study for finals while on Thanksgiving break.

Or she will be during breaks from partying with Tackett and his band. Having a brother who is an up-and-coming rockstar has its perks, and it also means she won't be alone since they're all staying here while I'm gone. I won't need to worry about her as I make my way east toward the stuffy, restricted, familiar obligations in New York.

At least while I'm at Berkeley, I have a sense of freedom, no matter how fleeting it may be.

"Your father and I will send the jet for you. What time do you plan to fly out?"

Oh, the shit is about to hit the fan.

"I don't need the jet, but thanks for offering." I hold my breath and wait for her reply.

"How do you plan to get home to New York from Berkeley if you don't take the jet? Surely, you don't intend to fly…commercial?" Mother scoffs, clearly deeply offended by the mere idea of flying commercial.

The woman is so out of touch with normal, everyday life that it's ridiculous.

"No, I have a ride." Silence lingers through the phone. "Mother? Are you there?"

"You don't intend to drive across the country by yourself. That's not safe, Athena, and I won't allow it."

Here we go.

"I never said that I was driving by myself."

"Who is riding with you? It doesn't matter. Absolutely not, Athena Rose Warren. This is unacceptable."

I sigh again, unable to contain my annoyance. "Mother, I'll be just fine."

I'm not a child, but Mother and Father seem to have a challenging time allowing their children any sense of freedom. I don't know how Artemis and Archimedes put up with this when they were my age.

At least Artie came to his senses and now practices law in North Carolina instead of helping Father at the senatorial offices and running Warren Enterprises Worldwide. He was smart enough to seek his freedom from this familial pressure cooker before his entire life got away from him. And while Archie may still be solidly in the Team Warren camp as acting CEO of the company, by marrying Blaire, he took a stand against the domination and put his foot down in a way I envy.

"Athena, I do *not* approve of this, and your father—"

"Will be fine. Mother, I'm sorry, but I have to go. I'll be home by Thanksgiving. Love you. I'll talk to you soon." I disconnect the call before she can issue any further protestations and drop my phone onto the couch beside me. "Talking to my mother is exhausting. I need a nap."

Valerie drops onto the couch next to me. "Who *are* you planning on riding home with?"

I chuckle and motion toward the messages on my screen. "I posted on the school carpool app and found someone going to New York."

She bursts out laughing and leans forward to read. "Your parents will lose their shit when they find out you're traveling across the country with a stranger."

"I think it makes me a terrible person, Valerie, but I sort of love that part of the plan." I glance at my watch. "And I have to go meet this guy and make sure he isn't a serial killer or something."

I grab my phone and keys and head toward the door to slip on my shoes.

"If I'm honest, I don't love this idea of yours, either, Athena."

"I'll be *fine*. I will call you every day and message you when we stop with proof-of-life texts. Deal?"

She shakes her head, sending her jet-black hair flying around her face. "I'm not convinced."

"Sorry. I'm not trying to make you uncomfortable, but at some point, my parents have to realize this is my life, and I intend to live it on my terms. If I take the family jet and come back at their beck and call, it only gives them the impression that what they do is okay. Besides, I need a few days to just have fun and be a normal college student before I'm subjected to the Warren mess."

"I understand, Athena." She shrugs. "It just makes me nervous."

"Noted." But it doesn't change my plan. If Mother thinks I'll simply roll over and fly home to spend a week with Cliff Clifton because she wants me to be the *one* Warren to marry "properly," she has another think coming. "Okay, I'm off to meet my ride. I'll be back in a bit."

"Good luck!"

I'm going to need it.

ISAIAH

Rolling into Berkeley, a bittersweet sense of finality settles over me.

This is it.

The end of the solo cross-country motorcycle trip I needed so badly is in sight. A few weeks without the day-to-day responsibilities and the chaos of Boston and all the expectations that exist there are finally over.

After a brief stop here to stretch my legs, hit the head, and grab some grub, it's on to Los Angeles for a few days to arrange to ship my bike back home before I need to board a plane and return to reality.

But now that I've hit the coast, I won't let what little time I have left go to waste. My final days of freedom will include the beach, some beer, and maybe a good hike. Soon enough, I'll be strapped to my desk again, clean-shaven, and these blissful moments will be long-forgotten memories.

I inhale a deep breath of the ocean-scented air and pull up outside what the neon sign tells me is Whiskey Jack's. Years of baking in the sun has made the old, dusty red paint covering the exterior peel away in places, but it looks like as good a place as any to stop.

It's been a long ride already today, and I'm in desperate need of a cold beer and a bathroom. I pull off my helmet and hang it on the handlebars before raking my hands through my hair and pulling on my favorite ball cap.

Just like me, it's seen better days.

This type of ride really does a number on the body, but it's all worth it to see the country and have this time alone. Plus, getting to stop in Colorado to see Bailey for the first time in years was a nice added bonus. Just like during our days together in the frat in college, spending time with him took my mind off all the stresses I tried to leave behind in Boston. It would have been amazing to take Route 66 instead of the northern route, to get to see all the amazing historical stops, but hitting Philly, Chicago, Wisconsin for some deep-fried cheese curds, then the tiny towns across South Dakota and Wyoming were just too much to pass up. Maybe the next trip I take—if I ever find the time to take one again—can follow that old path.

I tug open the door, and the smell of fried food and stale beer hits me. The place may be a dive, but it's exactly the kind of bar I would frequent if life were different. The sign for the bathrooms on the far wall catches my eye, and I make my way straight for them, twisting my shoulders to try to loosen the stiffness from my back due to too many hours on my bike today. Thankfully, it's nothing a cold beer and a bite of dinner can't fix.

And damn, does a beer sound good right now.

A couple would be even better, but if I want to get to L.A. tonight, I can't indulge as much as I would like.

I quickly take care of business and then twist on the faucet to wash my hands. A group of college guys hustles in laughing, and I'm transported to over a decade ago when my life was more straightforward, less complicated. Actually fun. I had no idea how easy I had it when I was in college.

Those were the days.

The guys have clearly had a few drinks and are doing nothing to keep their conversation private.

"Athena Warren, the heiress, is meeting you here tonight? I call bullshit. I don't believe you."

Athena Warren? Now there's a familiar name...

The young, skinny guy in a leather jacket steps up to the sink next to me and checks his dark hair in the mirror. "She'll be here. I checked the app and confirmed GoddessA is her." He glances back at his friends. "I guess you'll see when her sexy ass walks in here."

Laughter bounces off the cracked tile in the bathroom, and his buddies high-five him.

A short, blond guy shakes his head. "Yeah, only our Prez would get lucky enough to score an opportunity to drive Athena Warren home for a holiday."

"Hey, what can I say? I'm lucky like that, and I plan to get even *luckier,* if you know what I mean." He waggles his eyebrows and grins.

The jackass and his friends all laugh as they pull up

pictures of Athena on the internet and make lewd comments and innuendos about her. Anger churns the acid in my stomach as I finish washing my hands and leave the jerks in the bathroom.

What a bunch of idiots.

While I don't know the Warrens personally, they're a very prominent family on the East Coast. With her father a sitting senator from New York and her grandfather a former United States Supreme Court Justice, it would be impossible *not* to know the Warrens.

And the poor girl has no idea what she's walking into.

A sudden urge to warn her or somehow protect her from that douchebag tightens my fists at my sides as I grab a table by the window so I can keep an eye on my bike.

The waitress stops by the table, and I order my beer and look over the menu. But for some reason, I can't seem to let go of what those punks in the bathroom said about Athena Warren.

Why is she looking for a ride back to New York, anyway?

That family probably has half a dozen private jets they could send for her. But maybe she's just trying to have a typical college experience, and if anyone can relate to needing an escape from family pressure, it's me.

I take a sip of my beer, letting the cool, hoppy liquid parch my dry throat.

God, I needed this.

Even more after hearing those numbskulls. My hand tightens around the frosty glass just thinking about what they said again.

I have to do something.

Almost as if on cue, the front door swings open, and Athena Warren strolls in like she owns the place. She surveys her surroundings, entirely oblivious to the chatter surrounding her from the men and women alike whispering and stopping to take her in. Phones come out, snapping pictures, and she's so used to this by now, it doesn't even faze her. The Warrens are American royalty, so to have the princess show up here, of all places, is definitely a can't-miss photo opportunity.

Her gaze finally lands on me.

Damn.

I knew Athena was gorgeous. It would be impossible not to see it in every photo of her splashed across the tabloids. But in person, she's unreal. Her sleek black hair that settles just past her shoulders shimmers under the florescent overhead lighting, and her intense blue eyes rake over me with apparent interest. Full blood-red lips part as she smiles at me.

No doubt she's a stunner.

I grab the cold glass and take a sip to quench my suddenly dry throat, and Athena makes her way toward me.

She stops next to my table and pushes a strand of raven hair behind her diamond-studded ear. "Prez272?"

"What?"

Shit.

It comes to me quickly. Dark hair. Black leather jacket. Even though I'm a good decade older than that punk kid back there, she must think I'm him.

I clear my throat and force a half-smile. "Oh. Um, Prez? It's Isaiah. Are you the lady looking for a ride?"

No woman should have to hear what just went down in that bathroom. It would scare the shit out of her and make me seem creepy, too.

What the hell do I do?

She shifts nervously and glances around the bar. I stand and pull out a chair for her. Her ingrained manners kick in, and she smiles and graciously takes the seat, sending a clean, light, citrusy scent wafting over me.

Definitely sexy.

I haven't smelled much but dust, dirt, and leather for the last few weeks.

Sliding back in my chair, I clear my throat again. "So, Athena? Right? You're looking for a ride to New York?"

"Yes. Didn't you say you were headed that way? I thought that's why we were here, to finalize the ride share arrangement?"

"Yeah, yeah. I can give you a ride."

Where the hell did that come from?

After weeks on a cross-country trip, I had no intention of riding my bike back to the East Coast. I'll have to rearrange my whole damn schedule to do this—and piss off a lot of people who didn't want me to go in the first place.

I should just tell her what that kid said and let her call her parents to get a jet out here.

What in the hell is wrong with me?

Apparently, a lot of things. Because I don't tell her the truth. I can't. Not when I feel bad for this girl. If what the tabloids are saying is true, things in the Warren house are a mess because of her brothers. Artemis left the family business, and Archimedes just got married to his secretary—quite the scandal. Athena is the youngest child and likely feeling the pressure of everything her family expects of her.

A fun trip could be good for her. Let her see things she's probably never experienced before.

"Well, great!" She offers a smile that lights up her entire face, and something mischievous twinkles in her ocean-blue eyes. "This will be fun!"

My heart thunders against my ribcage in a way I haven't felt in a long time.

Shit. I am so fucked.

CHAPTER 2

ISAIAH

I roll up outside Athena's apartment, and for the millionth time since I agreed to this insane idea last night, I have to question my own sanity.

What the hell was I thinking?

A smart man would have come clean right away. But from our brief conversation over a beer at Whiskey Jack's, it was clear Athena is hell-bent on taking this cross-country journey, one way or another. Even if I had told her who I was —or in this case, wasn't—and what I overheard, she probably would have just posted looking for another ride, and something in me just won't let this girl climb into a car with someone who might have bad intentions.

And it's not like I flat-out *lied* to her. When she asked me to tell her about myself, I was honest. I am from Boston and am heading home for Thanksgiving. I just didn't mention that I'm not a student on break or that I'm not Prez272.

More of an omission than a lie, really. At least, that's what I'll keep telling myself. It's the only way I can ensure an honorable young lady doesn't get taken advantage of. For as worldly as Athena Warren may be in terms of places she's been on the family jet, I doubt she has much experience in the street smarts department.

I cut off my bike and remove my helmet just in time to watch Athena step from the front door of the complex in a pair of capris and a tank top, dragging a colossal suitcase that's not going to fit on this bike. I managed to condense all my shit over to one saddlebag last night and get my backpack strapped to the top of the trunk, but with the camping gear and a few supplies, there still isn't much room.

"Uh, good morning, Athena. I hate to tell you, but all of that"—I point to her suitcase, purse, and overnight bag—"isn't going to fit on this bike."

Her jaw drops, and she pushes her sunglasses up onto the top of her head. "You never said anything about a motorcycle."

I shrug and climb off my bike. "You never asked."

She glances between her bags and where I lean against the bike. "Are you kidding me? Where am I supposed to put my stuff?"

"In your house." I laugh, but she doesn't seem to find this situation as funny as I do, offering me an annoyed scowl in return. I tap on the saddlebag to my right. "I can give you this saddlebag."

A crease appears between her eyebrows. "That's it? Are you serious? That saddle...whatever you called it...wouldn't even hold *one* outfit, let alone a week's worth of clothes."

"It's all you've got. Make it work, Princess." I cross my arms over my chest.

She's accustomed to a particular lifestyle, but the sooner she realizes there will be no royal treatment from me and that traveling across the country on a motorcycle isn't easy, the better.

"Princess?" She rolls her eyes and huffs. "Fine. Give me a minute, *Bikes.*" She grates out the words between gritted teeth before turning and dragging her bags back inside.

Bikes?

I can already see this spoiled girl will be a handful.

Just keep telling yourself this was the right thing to do, Isaiah.

It's the only thing that will keep me sane for what is bound to be a very long trip. I pull out my phone and scan a flurry of text messages I'd rather ignore, and this trip is giving me the perfect excuse to put off returning to real life for another week or so.

A few minutes later, the door opens again, and Athena returns. I take in her trendy, fashionable biker jacket, full of zippers that probably aren't even functional. Her skin-tight designer jeans hug every sexy curve, and the knee-high boots with massive heels only accentuate her shape.

Damn.

No doubt she has the best items that money can buy, from head to toe. But it's all wrong. Her outfit is something she *thinks* a biker should wear, not what is actually appropriate for the journey we're about to embark on.

She dangles a smaller bag and a backpack from her hands. "Is this better?"

Fuck if I'm about to waste an opportunity to openly appreciate this woman. I scan her from her shiny black hair to the heeled boots on her feet. Athena Warren is sexy.

"Much." I take her bags from her and drop them beside the bike, so I can fish out the helmet I grabbed for her last night on my way to the hotel—a last-minute booking I had to make when I realized I wasn't going to make it to L.A. as planned.

None of this is according to plan.

But it feels like it's too late to go back now.

"Here." I offer the helmet to her. "Put this on."

"You got me a helmet." She raises a dark eyebrow at me. "A *pink* helmet? Are you kidding me?" Athena looks disgusted for a second, but then she manages to regain that Warren composure and forces a fake smile. "I mean, thank you."

"It's girly. You don't like it?" I pull the half-shell helmet from her hand and settle it on top of her head before fastening the strap under her chin.

Shit. She smells good.

Her blue eyes assess me from under the ridiculous pink helmet.

Shit. It is ridiculous. What was I thinking?

"We can stop and get you another one."

"No." She shakes her head. "This one is fine. Thank you."

Standing this close to check that the strap is secure but not too tight, I almost drown in her gaze.

All the work shit that has been weighing on me floats away on the blue waves there. The fact that I should have my ass on a plane headed back home to Boston in a few hours and not be about to drive this young woman to New York seems irrelevant.

None of it seems as vital as it did yesterday, for some reason.

"You ever ride on a motorcycle before, Athena?"

My money is on no. I'm pretty sure the Warren family wouldn't allow their princess to do something so "reckless" and "dangerous."

She squares her shoulders and huffs, placing her hands on her hips. "Yes. Of course, I have."

Lie.

I don't believe that for a second, but I am not about to call her out on it, either. Not when all of this started with my lying to her. If she doesn't want to admit she's a motorcycle virgin, then she's going to suffer the consequences.

"This is a very hard drive, especially for someone who isn't used to riding. We have several long days ahead of us."

It's a warning to her as much as to myself. I have a feeling this is going to be one long trip—for a myriad of reasons.

ATHENA

There's no way in hell that I'll let Isaiah know I've never ridden a motorcycle before.

If he backs out of giving me a ride home, I won't have the time to try to find another ride. And I'm not about to call Mother and Father and ask them to send the jet. I'd much rather risk my ass being a little sore than have to do *that*.

Besides, I'm starting to suspect that he needs my help financially to get back home. Paying for college must take all his money because he barely has any belongings on this dusty, dirty, beat-up bike.

What if these meager things are all he has? That's sad.

I let my gaze drift over him. His dark, wavy hair—freed from the confines of the ratty baseball cap he was wearing last night—could use a cut, and his angular, stubble-covered jaw looks like he hasn't shaved in a few days. The leather jacket that moves with him almost like a second skin appears well-worn and loved, just as much as the jeans that hug his perfect thighs and ass and the dusty boots on his feet.

He may be destitute, but I would never judge someone for that. Not the way Mother and Father would.

Which gives me an idea...

He's the perfect decoy—a fake date to keep my parents from hooking me up with Cliff Clifton—or whoever else Mother comes up with—while I'm at home. Isaiah is everything they'd hate and then some.

He's perfect. Now, I only have to convince him to go along with it once we hit New York.

His mossy-green eyes meet mine, and his lips twitch. He totally busted me checking him out. "This is a very hard drive, especially for someone who isn't used to riding. We have several long days ahead of us."

The warning comes in such a fatherly tone, I'm really starting to feel the age difference here. He must have come back to school to get a degree with a few years off after high school. Still, the warning raises my annoyance and the hairs on the back of my neck.

Jesus, how hard can it be to sit on the back of a bike for a few hundred miles a day?

He's making it seem like I'm some sort of lightweight who can't handle this. I'll show him that he doesn't need to worry about me.

I got this.

"I'll be fine. Thank you for your concern."

But one thing I will absolutely *not* be doing is camping with the gear he has strapped to the bike. Maybe I can talk him into staying at hotels. I don't mind paying. It's the least I can do, but something about him tells me he's a proud man, and he may not appreciate what he would see as charity.

I slide my sunglasses up on my nose and walk around Isaiah before he can reply. He offers a little huffed laugh and bends down to stow my things. Maybe I take a quick peek of his rock-hard backside, but I'm only human, and this man was made to be looked at.

Not that I will be telling him that. Men don't need to have their overinflated egos stroked.

While he finishes readying the gear, I stare at the metal monster on the street.

How the hell do you get on this thing?

I definitely can't ask since I just lied and said I've ridden before.

How hard can it really be?

Isaiah comes around the motorcycle, and with practiced ease, he straddles it, grabs his helmet from its perch on the handlebars, and tosses it onto his head before firing up the bike.

That shouldn't be so hot.

The rumble of the growly engine vibrates the ground, and excitement I hadn't anticipated jolts through my limbs. I've never driven across the country, let alone had the opportunity to ride on a motorcycle. Both would be frowned upon by the Warrens, and while I've never been one to fold to everything Mother and Father want, as long as I'm still in school, I need their help.

Once I graduate, it'll be a different story. The birthday money I've been having Archie help me invest should be enough for me to break free from them and start my own life without the cloud of expectation hanging over me.

"Hop on, Athena," Isaiah jerks his chin behind him while he leans the bike to the side enough to knock up the kickstand.

He makes it sound so easy.

Here goes nothing.

I inhale a deep breath of his leathery scent to calm my nerves before placing my hand on his shoulder. His firm, muscular shoulder. Then, I hike up my leg and swing it over the seat just like I watched him do moments ago.

But somehow, my other foot leaves the ground.

SHIT!

I frantically cling to Isaiah's shoulder as I topple off the side of the bike. The pavement below races up at me quickly, but a strong arm wraps around my waist and pulls me upright, saving me from falling while simultaneously keeping the bike upright.

Shit! That's embarrassing.

He turns his head toward me and yells over the engine, "Are you okay?"

I finally get my left foot back underneath me, with my right leg resting across the seat of the motorcycle so I'm in a semi split.

"Yeah, I must have slipped."

And lost my dignity right along with my footing.

Embarrassment heats my cheeks, and I manage to right myself and get seated on this damn two-wheel death machine.

Maybe this wasn't my greatest idea.

But he made it look so easy.

Isaiah laughs. "Put your feet on the floorboards and your arms around my waist. You need to hang on until you get used to this."

I settle against the small backrest and find a good position for my feet. Though not the most comfortable way to travel, it isn't as bad as I imagined it could be when he gave his warning. I follow his instruction and wrap my arms around his midsection.

He stiffens momentarily, almost like he isn't expecting my touch even though he's the one who told me to do it. Then he relaxes slightly and maneuvers the bike to point it toward the road, his muscles tightening and bunching under his jacket with every movement.

I cling to him to ensure I don't fall off this bike again.

Mortifying!

One of his big, warm hands slides over the top of mine, where it rests against his stomach, and he gives it a gentle squeeze. "Hang on tight."

Gripping even tighter, he pats my hand again.

Okay, maybe this isn't as bad as I thought.

Having my arms wrapped around him feels almost

natural. Not a bad way to spend a week or so making our way across the country.

He releases my hand, reaches for the handlebars, and revs the engine.

Oh hell, that's sexy. He's sexy.

Everything on my body vibrates, and I squeeze Isaiah, my entire body tingling with anticipation for us to take off. He gives the bike some gas and we peel away from the curb.

"Shiiiiiiit!" I squeal and cling to him like my life depends on it.

Because it does.

Fear grips my chest, stealing my breath as the howling wind whips around us, but it's quickly replaced by my heart thudding for a wholly new reason. Everything I see every day looks completely different, new somehow. Everything is so much more…alive.

Mother and Father will lose their shit when they see me pull up at the house on a motorcycle.

They'll be furious that I rode across America on the back of a potentially homeless stranger's bike. Then they'll probably have coronaries when I bring him in as my Thanksgiving date—assuming he agrees to that by the time we get to New York.

I laugh out loud at my lunacy, the sound immediately sucked up and pulled away by the wind, but really, it's kind of brilliant. He's the opposite of everything my parents expect for my partner.

It's almost too perfect.

And to think, I gave Archie shit for this same idea when he was going to marry a woman he found in the classifieds. It's actually brilliant and might buy me some time with my parents and their scheming, match-making ways—at least for Thanksgiving.

Cliff Clifton or bad-ass biker Isaiah? Is there even a choice?

CHAPTER 3

ATHENA

Oh, my God!

My ass is literally numb. But surprisingly, that somehow still doesn't stop it from hurting like a bitch.

I wiggle uncomfortably on the seat of this bike for the thousandth time in minutes. It's shocking Isaiah can even hold this thing upright with how much I'm squirming back here. He doesn't strike me as the type to do much complaining, though, thank God.

After hours on the road, the high speeds of the highway, the wind whipping me around, and the fact that I am new to riding are all taking their toll. I can't even remember the last time I was this tired or dirty.

I'd kill for a hot bath.

The nine and a half hours he said it would take to get from Berkeley to Vegas didn't seem that long when we started at six this morning. But after the last time we stopped, I didn't want to get back on. Not with the way every

23

muscle and bone in my body was screaming at me to stay off the mechanical beast.

It was the sheer willpower and stubbornness all Warrens are born with that made me climb back on. What was fun for the first few hours has turned into my own version of Hell. And here I thought that would be Thanksgiving break with Cliff Clifton. My butt bones feel like they are tearing through my flesh, and I'm pretty sure I never knew an ass could ache like this, let alone ever experienced it myself before.

I can't believe I have *days* of sitting on this damn bike ahead of me. That private jet Mother offered to send is looking better and better.

This was a terrible idea.

And, of course, to add insult to injury, I need to pee. Every vibration from the road and bump we hit just reminds me of how badly.

I tap Isaiah on the shoulder and try to yell over the noise surrounding us. "I need to stop."

But he can't hear me. The bike, the excessive wind, and high speeds makes communicating hard. He cocks his head to the side, trying to hear me better but not taking his eyes off the road.

"What?" he shouts over the roar.

"I need you to stop at a gas station." Although I'm yelling louder, my words still don't reach even my own ears.

He taps his helmet and shakes his head, so it's no use. Still, he slows and motions that he's going to stop on the side of the highway. It isn't a surprise, really. I'm sure he wants to make sure I'm okay. He's been exceptionally kind today and has gone out of his way to stop more than I'm sure he normally would to give me extra breaks.

I hang on for dear life as he pulls off onto the shoulder, then leans the bike to the side so he can extend the kickstand down with his foot. This new angle only makes my ass scream in protest more.

Isaiah kills the engine and taps my leg to tell me to hop off. But as bad as I hurt sitting here, the idea of standing sounds even worse.

Shit. I'm not sure I can get off this bike, let alone that my legs will hold me up if I do.

He taps my leg again, and I huff.

"Okay, fine. Give me a minute."

The bastard laughs, but I can't worry about him while my butt is broken.

I slide off the bike slowly, my foot hits the rocky, uneven ground, and with every ounce of strength I can muster, I swing my other leg over the seat. "Ow, ow, ow. Why does this hurt so bad?"

Almost two decades of riding horses, and I've never *once* had this type of pain. I'd rather be thrown from that feisty Arabian out at the barn than have to sit on this hunk of metal again.

Isaiah smirks at me, and somehow, it makes him more handsome, even as it also makes me want to smack him. "I told you it's a long ride, especially when you're not used to it. We aren't far from Vegas. Think you can make it a few more hours if I stop and let you stretch a few times?"

Oh, Jesus, he said hours, didn't he?

"Yeah, but can we stop somewhere to use the bathroom?" I *really* need to go, but scanning around us, all I find is the vast, endless, barren desert that only makes my body ache even more.

If Vegas isn't even in sight, that means it's a *long* ride ahead of us before we can stop for the night. I lean forward and rest my palms on my thighs, stretching my back and my ass, shifting from side to side.

Ugghhhh...I could cry.

It hurts and feels amazing at the same time. But I won't let any tears fall and give Isaiah the satisfaction of seeing me break down.

Why in the hell did I wear these boots with heels?

My calves are killing me from the hours in this elevated position. The first order of business when we get to Vegas—after a hot bath and a drink—is to get some new riding gear, or else I might not make the rest of this trip. And caving to Mother and calling for a flight home, or even going commercial, seems like the greater of the two evils despite how much pain I'm in right now.

"Well, I hate to be the bearer of bad news, but according to my app, there's no restroom around for a while. About an hour away, from the looks of it."

Cars honk at us as they fly by at super-fast speeds—but whether that's some sort of "biker" thing or because I'm bent over in skin-tight jeans and four-inch-heeled boots, wiggling my ass back and forth, I can't really be sure.

What I *am* sure of is that my bladder isn't making it another hour with the jostling of that motorcycle. "I can't wait that long. So, what am I supposed to do?"

Isaiah smiles in that smug way I'm beginning to learn is a foreshadowing of news that I'm not going to like—but that he finds entirely amusing.

Asshole.

"I guess you'll have to go over there behind that scrubby brush and let nature take its course." He hitches a thumb over his shoulder, and I look where he's pointing.

Cars whizzing by and a tiny thicket not far from the road is my only option? No way.

"You're kidding, right?" I force myself to stand fully again, issuing a low groan of protest at the stab of pain in my back. "You can't be serious?"

"I'm absolutely serious. It's gonna happen more than once

on this trip, you know. We're going to be taking Route 66 after Vegas, and it's pretty barren in several stretches. You might as well get used to it now."

I can't *go* in nature. This is crazy...I can barely go to the bathroom with other people in a public restroom with me.

"I suggest you pick out a bush and get to work. We want to get to Vegas before it gets to be too late because we have to leave early again tomorrow morning. We both need the rest." Isaiah points out toward the bushes that are a sorry excuse for a bathroom.

I really didn't think this trip through. Karma must be trying to screw me over for trying to rile up Mother and Father. I could've been on a damn private jet, but no, I had to "stick it to the man."

Big mistake, apparently.

Lesson learned, Karma. I got the fucking memo.

"Do you at least have any tissues I can use?"

Seriously, I need *some* creature comforts or I will never make it a few more hours, let alone the almost week it will take to get all the way to New York on this thing.

"Unless you intend to dig a hole and bury it, no, you can't use a tissue. It's not like I have a trash bag on my bike. And you can't litter." The corners of his perfect lips twitch again. "You could stick it in your pocket, I suppose."

He's so damn smug.

Hot and smug and rotten, and I hate that he's right. *And* that I have to pee basically in front of a handsome, homeless stranger. I hate that I have to pee behind a bush that barely even qualifies as one on the side of the damn highway in the middle of nowhere and I can't wipe. I hate that my butt hurts, and I'm going to have to squat, in heels, in the desert, with a sore ass.

Why did I even decide to go on this damned journey in the first place?

Standing up to the Warrens suddenly seems a lot less important...

I release a heavy sigh and point at Isaiah. "I tell you what, when we get to Vegas, I'm renting the fanciest damn hotel room there is, and I don't want to hear one complaint about it. I'll pay for you. Just get me out of here and to *there* as quickly as possible."

"I don't need your charity, Princess." He practically spits the words at me. "I can pay my own way."

"Is that a complaint, Bikes? What did I just say?"

"Don't call me Bikes."

"Don't call me Princess."

He started it with that nonsense.

I scan the desert, locate the nearest thicket of bushes that might be heavy enough to even remotely conceal me from the traffic or my road trip partner, and grumble the entire time as I make my way over there and drop my pants to the sound of Isaiah's unwanted laughter.

"I'm so happy that you find this amusing, Bikes," I shout sarcastically.

"I really do, *Princess*."

I knew it! He is an asshole!

Watch me get bit on the ass by a scorpion. That'd be just my luck.

ISAIAH

Who would have ever thought Athena would turn out to be pretty damn normal?

Definitely not me.

Surprising and refreshing.

I had anticipated *true* princess behavior the entire ride

today, yet she's sucked up what I know must be a lot of discomfort. Still, she definitely has her limits, and peeing on the side of a desert highway is apparently one of them.

She's a trooper, though. Taking care of business, literally. Behind bushes that don't really hide much, so I avert my gaze to be the gentleman Mother raised all her boys to be.

My phone beeps with a message, and I check it, thankful for the distraction from a half-naked Athena. Until I see who it's from…

James: Hey, big bro! You get your bike set up to ship home? Return flight still set for tomorrow?

Shit.

I should have known I wouldn't be able to slip a change of plans past the twins, as much as I would have loved to get a few more days without them hounding me. There is far too much going on right now for them to not be up my ass about when I'll be back. Father, too. Though, I think he understands my need for downtime better than James or Jacob. Those two are still young enough to think overworking themselves won't come back to bite them after a few years.

Naïve idiots.

They haven't learned anything from watching Dad and me and seeing how worn down we get. But once they hit thirty, they'll get it. That's about the time I realized I needed to slow down, or I would give myself a coronary. Still, it took another two years for me to make this trip; two years during which I only worked myself harder and pushed myself to the breaking point.

A few more days without me won't kill them.

Hopefully.

They may tear each other apart without me to referee their spats, but I'll leave that in Father's capable hands. I have something more important to worry about—getting the girl currently pissing in the bushes back to New York unharmed.

Isaiah: Change of plans. I'm driving the bike back. See you in a week or so. You and Jacob try not to burn anything down before I get back.

Jacob: You're changing your plans and taking another week off? Is this a sign to let us know you've been kidnapped? Will there be a ransom?

Little shit.

He isn't wrong, though.

The control freak in me means I rarely take vacations, and I definitely don't change my plans. But I never expected to run into the Athena Warren debacle, either. And while James and Jacob may pester me and get on my nerves, I know they have things reliably well in hand while I'm gone for a few weeks. Otherwise, I never would have left in the first place. I wouldn't do that to Father, not when he depends on me so heavily.

James: Don't worry, Jacob. Isaiah will likely micromanage the kidnapping and have the kidnappers following his orders before long. He's got this.

I bark out a laugh because he isn't wrong. This trip has been a break from that for me, but if some asshole did try to do something stupid like kidnap me, I would likely come out on top—just like I always do.

Even though this time away has been incredible, the worrier in me still thinks about everything I'm potentially missing back home—with the business *and* with Dad. He isn't a young man anymore, and ever since Mom died, it's been a struggle keeping him on task at times. It made leaving all the harder, but the old man practically shoved me out the door because he understood I *needed* it.

Isaiah: How is everything? Dad doing good? I tried to call him yesterday and check in but didn't get an answer.

Jacob: All good. Aunt Jenny came into town to visit Dad. She's giving him a run for his money. He can't keep up with her anymore. She was dragging him to brunch for mimosas, so they are likely hung over today.

James: All good on the work front, too. About to head into the big meeting you ditched. Cross your fingers we land this account.

We could really use it, and that makes the timing of my road trip even more troublesome to the entire family.

Isaiah: I can't believe I left you two shits in charge of this. Don't screw it up.

They won't. They are more than capable of handling the day-to-day operations. I just needed to let go of control long enough for all of us to realize it. This vacation was the perfect opportunity.

Jacob: We got this, old man! Go have some fun before your dick stops working. Safe trip, bro!

James: I'll hit you up after and let you know how it went.

"That was a whole new lesson in humility." Athena

chuckles and reaches in the saddlebag that contains her stuff to grab hand sanitizer.

I tuck away my phone and grin at her. "Nothing quite as humbling as pissing along the side of a highway, Princess."

She offers me a scowl that somehow does nothing to reduce the beauty of her perfect bow lips. "You're not funny, and stop calling me Princess, Bikes!"

Clearly annoyed, she pulls out her phone, holds it up and snaps and selfie, then rapidly taps at the screen.

"What are you doing?"

She flips the phone toward me to show the text she just sent.

PROOF OF LIFE: JUST TOOK A PISS IN THE DESERT ON OUR WAY TO VEGAS! WITHOUT TOILET PAPER!

I chuckle again, which earns me another dirty look. "Who are you sending that to?"

"My best friend, Val. She demanded proof-of-life texts at each stop, or she's going to call the cops."

Smart.

She releases a long, heavy sigh, slips her phone back into her pocket, and points at me. "When we get to Vegas, I'm ordering an insane amount of room service and taking the world's longest bath. What about you?"

"Definitely could eat. I need to look at our route for tomorrow and check the bike over before we head back out to make sure everything is ready to go. Any ideas where you want to stay?"

"Yeah, can we stop at the Drakeston?"

I chuckle and shake my head. Of course, the princess wants the most expensive and exclusive hotel on the Strip. "Yeah, that's fine."

"To the Drakeston!" Athena shouts and pumps her fist, the action reminding me how young she really is.

But even though she's almost a full decade my junior, the

girl has shown she's a lot stronger and wiser than I gave her credit for. This time, when she straps on her helmet, it goes far quicker than the last time. The setting sun turns her hair shades of auburn and a blue-black I don't think I've ever seen before.

She really is stunning.

And I should not *be thinking that about my road trip partner.*

Definitely not.

I strap on my helmet, straddle the bike, and fire it up. "To the Drakeston, Princess!"

Athena's laugh travels through the air over the roar of my bike, and I can't contain my smile. It feels good and foreign all at once. I've been so caught up with work over the last few years, I've about forgotten what fun and freedom feel like.

I guess I can thank Athena for this reminder.

Athena grumbles incoherently as she straddles the bike again, managing to keep herself upright this time, despite how sore she must be. She wraps her arms around me and taps my chest, which sends a little rush of heat spreading through me.

She's ready to go.

And I'm in trouble.

We ride in silence, the wind lashing around us, the purr of the engine and noise of the road filling our ears. As this beautiful woman hangs on to me, a peace settles over me, a sense of calm I haven't felt in ages. Not even on the solo leg of my journey that I had thought was so good for my soul.

Hell, maybe I really did need to extend my vacation just a bit longer.

CHAPTER 4

ATHENA

Oh, thank God!

I've never been so happy to see a hotel in my entire life. The lobby gleams under the beautiful crystal chandeliers dangling from the ceilings that must be at least three stories high, and despite all the privileges being a Warren has provided me, all the beautiful places I've traveled to in my life, I can't remember ever seeing anything so stunning.

Though maybe it's the thought of finally getting horizontal and resting my sore butt that makes it so appealing.

We approach the front desk, every step I take sending knives of pain into my sore feet and stabs into my poor ass.

A blonde with bright-blue eyes and a massive smile that's directed squarely at my dusty, grimy, dirty, hot companion says, "Welcome to the Drakeston. How may I help you this evening?"

Really, I can't say I blame her.

While I look like I've been dragged from Berkeley to Las

Vegas behind the motorcycle, Isaiah appears made for this lifestyle. All stubbly, chiseled jaw and soft, kissable lips. Leather-encased bad-ass biker. Somehow, our spin on that two-wheel ass-breaker made him look even better.

How the hell is that fair?

"Yeah"—I slide my credit card across the counter—"I'd like to get two rooms, please."

Isaiah turns toward me and holds up a hand in protest. "What exactly do you think you're doing there, Princess?"

I peek up at him, ignoring the inquisitive look from the front desk girl, who appears a little too interested in the fact that I'm requesting separate rooms. "I'm getting us a place to rest. It's the least I can do since I can't help drive."

He shakes his head. "You don't need to do that. I can pay for our rooms."

That's awfully sweet that he at least offered, but I'm confident this hotel is way out of his budget. It is for most people. And it will be for me once I'm off the Warren payroll. Might as well use the credit card while I can, before I graduate and get cut off when I tell Mother and Father that I'm not coming back to New York and won't be getting married to anyone they set me up with.

Staying in California just feels right, and if they know I'm considering going to law school to become a public defender instead of to represent Warren Enterprises Worldwide and help Archie run the company, they're sure to cut this thing up faster than they cut Artemis out of the will when he quit.

I can't let Isaiah spend more than most people make in a week on one night in this hotel just because it's where I want to stay. "No, really, Isaiah, I insist."

He holds up his hands in surrender and raises a dark eyebrow. "Okay, if you insist. How can I say no?"

His chuckle suggests something is funny, but whatever the

joke is, it goes right over my head. Or maybe he's totally lost his shit. Maybe we spent too long on the bike today. Maybe the sun cooked his brain in that sleek *black* helmet of his. And maybe I'm still not over the fact that this man bought me a *pink* helmet. This big, burly guy with the perfect ass for a pair of jeans picked out a *pink* helmet for me like I'm some little girl.

Princess, my ass.

The concierge clicks around on the keyboard for a few moments, and I take the opportunity to snap a selfie and fire it off to Val with the message ***PROOF OF LIFE: MADE IT TO THE DRAKESTON IN VEGAS*** before the concierge finally actually looks at me.

"Oh! Oh, my goodness! You're Athena Warren!" Her cheeks redden with embarrassment. "Miss Warren, my apologies that I didn't recognize you sooner. I'm sorry to have to tell you this, but there's a paleontologist conference here, and well, we only have one room available, and that's the honeymoon suite."

Oh, for fuck's sake. Of course, there's only one room.

Isaiah motions toward the woman. "Go ahead, Athena, take the room. I'll sleep down here in the lobby or just go grab my bike and camp. No big deal."

Somehow, I just know he's serious. He would totally do that because, in the short amount of time that I've known Isaiah, he's proven to be a gentleman. Despite laughing at my misery from the ride and having to piss in the desert.

But I can't seriously let him do that. "We'll take the room, please."

Isaiah doesn't interfere or ask any questions about what our sleeping arrangements might be. And thank God for that because I have no idea. The only things at the forefront of my mind are a long, hot bath and a big pile of one of everything from room service.

I need to wash off all this nature. Everything else will work itself out.

The blonde finalizes the paperwork, and I almost shed a tear the moment I get the key card in my hand. "Top floor, you'll need to use your key card to access it in the elevator."

"Thank you." I force a smile, take my credit card back from her, and stash it in my purse.

Isaiah grabs my bag and starts toward the elevator. I stumble after him on still-unsteady legs and try to grab my meager luggage, but he isn't having it.

He shakes his head and winks at me. "I've got it, Princess."

No sense in arguing. He doesn't seem the type to change his mind about much, and honestly, I'm not sure I have the energy left to drag that thing anyway.

"Thank you, *Bikes.*" I put extra emphasis on his new nickname since he continues to call me Princess despite my protests.

A low, sexy laugh rumbles from his chest, and he glances back at me. His green eyes meet mine, and his full, pink lips tilt in a slight smile. My breath hitches in my chest. He holds eye contact just a half-second too long, like he's taking in the most beautiful thing he's seen all day and wants to memorize it. And with just that one look, goosebumps break out all over my skin.

Crap.

He focuses forward and pushes the button for the elevator while I shake my head to try to clear away the very dangerous thoughts I almost had.

It's just my imagination. Too many hours spent hanging on to this man to keep myself on his bike.

And God, is he allllll man.

My eyes drift down to the way his jeans hug his ass.

The elevator doors open with a gentle chime, finally

breaking the trance I have no right to be in over a much older man I barely know.

Isaiah motions for me to go first. I clear my throat and try to gather my thoughts before I enter the elevator, stick the keycard into the slot, and press the button for the top floor.

Was that all just in my head?

Isaiah doesn't seem affected at all by that little *exchange* we just had. He follows me in and moves to stand to my side and slightly behind me. Heat radiates off him, and the tiny space suddenly feels even smaller, like it's closing in on us and pushing me even closer to him. I've never been more aware of my appearance or someone else's presence in my entire life.

He shifts slightly, and his arm brushes against mine, sending a little electric jolt up and through my body. I clear my throat again and fight the urge to glance back at him.

Why the hell does this feel so damn awkward?

I've never been shy a day in my life. Since the day I was born and given the Warren name, I've been on the world's stage, gawked at like a zoo animal, and photographed just about everywhere. I've literally spent *all day* with my legs and arms wrapped around this man, but somehow, standing here in this elevator, knowing we're about to share a room for the night, makes my legs shake more than the damn motorcycle did.

The closer we come to hitting our floor and getting out of this elevator, the tighter my body seems to wind until I'm practically vibrating. A ding announces our arrival, and the doors slide open.

Isaiah motions again for me to go ahead of him—always the gentleman.

Or maybe he just wants to look at my ass?

It's not like I haven't been doing it to him, too. I would try to sashay a little bit, give him a bit of a show, but my legs, feet, and ass hurt so bad right now, I can barely hobble, let alone do anything remotely playful or sexy.

Why the hell do I want to do anything sexy *at all?*

That's something I have zero energy to explore right now. Not when I'm so dang close to finally getting out of these boots and lying down.

The door to our room stands just outside the elevator, and I slide the key card into the lock and wait for the beep. Isaiah reaches out and turns the handle, holding the door so I can enter in front of him. Someone definitely taught him manners. At least…some. I doubt whoever it was would have appreciated him enjoying my humiliating myself by squatting in the desert.

But the view of the Strip through the floor-to-ceiling windows straight ahead draws me away from him and from considering what the hell is happening between us any further.

While I've stayed at this hotel several times, I've never been in the honeymoon suite. And this view is the best one by far—one meant to be enjoyed in the hot tub and small pool set out on the balcony.

Isaiah sets down my bag by the dresser. "Wow! Great view."

I turn back toward him and watch as he scans the room. This must be a real shock for him—such an expensive, opulent space he can't be used to. He opens each of the doors then shuts them quickly, examining every nook and cranny of the massive room and attached bathroom.

He steps out and runs a hand back through his dark, wavy hair. "Okay, Athena, get rested up and I'll meet you down in the lobby at five o'clock in the morning. We gotta get an early start."

"Meet me? Wait…you're not going to stay here?"

"No. There's only one bed and one room. Of course, I'm

not going to stay here. I told you, I'll stay in the lobby. If that gets too loud, I'll find a spot and camp out with my bike. Either way, I'll be here to pick you up at five."

He's serious?

This man who has driven us—me—around all day would go sleep in the dirt before shacking up with me...

Should I be impressed by what a gentleman he's being or be offended?

Regardless of his reason for it, it's stupid for him to even suggest sleeping in the damn lobby or *camping* after that ride. "Don't be ridiculous, Isaiah. Just stay here. You need to rest, too. You need a shower and dinner. One of us can just sleep on the couch tonight."

He rubs his large fingers along the scruff on his chin while he contemplates my offer.

Why is that so sexy?

His warm emerald gaze meets mine, and he raises a dark eyebrow at me. "Are you sure? I really don't want to impose. I don't want to make you feel uncomfortable."

Damn.

He really is a nice guy—a nice, sexy-as-hell guy who is making me feel all kinds of uncomfortable but not because he's done anything wrong.

"Don't be silly. You're staying, I insist."

I have to turn and look out the windows toward the balcony just to clear the unwanted thoughts from my head. That hot tub looks so damn inviting. All those jets and scalding water working on my aching muscles sounds absolutely divine right now. Except, I don't have a bathing suit.

Crap.

ISAIAH

Athena stands in front of the windows, and she releases a heavy sigh, her shoulders sagging in resignation. Even with all the pain she's been in from the long ride and the completely inappropriate shoes, she's kept things upbeat the entire day. Now, she just looks defeated.

I move to stand beside her, ignoring the beautiful view to focus on the frown on her perfect bow lips. "What's wrong?

Another long, slow sigh slips over to me. "I really want to get in that hot tub, but because of you and your stupid storage-less motorcycle, I didn't get to bring a bathing suit."

She casts an annoyed glare in my direction, but the corner of her mouth twitches, demonstrating her sense of humor is still solidly intact.

Barking out a laugh, I shake my head. "I mean, you can always just get naked, Athena. I promise not to look." I cross my fingers in front of my chest where she can clearly see them. "Much."

This time, she's the one releasing a ridiculously loud and obnoxious laugh. "Yeah, you're real funny, Bikes." She grins and shrugs. "But I *do* have on a bra and panties. It's not that different from a bikini, right?"

"Uh…" Visions of Athena in nothing but a lacy bra and tiny panties flash in my head. "Nope."

Shit. It definitely is.

She smiles and pulls off her dusty jacket, letting it fall unceremoniously onto the plush carpet. "Well, in that case, I'm going in."

"It will be good for all your sore muscles."

Athena nods and watches me expectantly, though I have no idea what she's waiting for. After a moment of awkward silence, she raises a dark eyebrow at me and smirks.

"What?"

She lifts her hand and spins her finger in a circle. "Turn around so I can get undressed."

"Oh! Sorry."

Shit.

I turn my back to her, facing the far wall, but a flicker of movement in my peripheral vision draws my attention that way.

Athena's reflection in the windows…

Her hands at the hem of her shirt…

Perfect pale skin as she pulls it up and over her head, exposing a black, lacy bra…

Shit. Shit. Shit.

I squeeze my eyes closed, scrape my hands against my growing beard, and inhale a deep breath to try not to react to what I just caught a glimpse of. She's right. It isn't that different than what most women wear to a beach or a pool, but I couldn't help but notice the way her nipples pebbled beneath the dark material.

But I was raised to respect women.

Even though there's definitely some tension between us, something unlike I've ever felt with another woman, I'm not about to disregard her boundaries and watch her when she asked me not to.

Christ, if she's wearing a thong...

Nope. Not going to think about that.

I take several more deep, cleansing breaths while the sounds of rustling clothing taunt me from behind. Two loud thunks make me jump and whirl toward her. "What the hell was that?"

Athena busts out laughing, her hand at the button of her jeans. "Um, I tossed my boots and they hit the bed frame."

My rapidly beating heart slows for a split second until what I'm staring at registers. "Oh, shit." I slap my hand over my eyes and turn around again. "Sorry, I—"

She laughs, the sound light and seductive. "Don't worry about it. It's basically just a swimsuit, right?"

I clear my throat. "Yeah, right."

Her jeans hit the floor just behind me. "Why don't you order us some room service and then come join me?"

Join her?

I hadn't even thought about it. After the day we've had, I figured she'd want to relax out there alone while I took a shower or something. "Uh, I hadn't planned on coming in."

"You may not need it as badly as I do, but don't tell me those jets won't feel incredible after the ride we had today."

Hell yes, they will.

But getting into a hot tub with a mostly naked Athena Warren sounds *very* dangerous.

Before I can answer, a knock sounds on the door, making me jump again. I look toward the door and glance over my shoulder at Athena.

She quirks a brow as if to say, "You want me to get it?"

I chuckle and try to avoid gawking at her in her bra and panties while I motion toward the door. "I've got it."

Athena doesn't flinch; she just turns and saunters out toward the balcony.

Shit. A thong.

For a girl who wanted me to turn around while she changed, she doesn't seem to care very much that I'm seeing her like this.

It's just a swimsuit.

I'll keep telling myself that as many times as I need to tonight. Probably a million.

I make my way to the door and check the peephole to find a concierge with a cart in the hallway.

What the hell?

I tug it open. "Can I help you?"

He grins at me. "Good evening, sir. Compliments of the

house for Miss Warren. It's always a pleasure to have her stay with us."

"Thanks, just leave the cart. I'll bring it in."

"Oh, my gosh! This feels *soooo* good." Athena purrs and moans out on the balcony, and if I didn't know better, I'd say she just got off.

The concierge *doesn't* know better; that's evident by the bright-red blush that spreads over his face. "Okay, sir, have a lovely evening. Should you or Miss Warren require anything during your stay, my number is on this card. I am available for your needs, around the clock."

He turns to leave, but Athena's comment about my storage-less motorcycle floats around my head. "Wait, can you get our clothes laundered and back to us before we leave early tomorrow morning?"

Athena doesn't have much to wear. Neither do I, but it's different for women. I can't deny that. I'll stop and get her properly outfitted, but until then, it never hurts to have an extra change of clothes while on the road.

"Of course, sir. My pleasure. I can come in and retrieve the items, or I can wait here. There's a laundry bag in the bathroom."

I peek over my shoulder and just catch a glimpse of Athena's firm ass as she slips all the way into the hot tub. Another loud moan pours from her lips.

Hell no, he isn't coming in here.

"Wait right here." I grab the cart and pull it inside before shutting the door.

"Who is it, Isaiah?"

Now fully submerged, my name comes out of her mouth as a content groan, and fuck if that doesn't make my cock twitch.

"The concierge. He's brought some food and drinks. I'm going to give him our clothes to wash, okay? I'll leave you a shirt of mine to put on when you get out of the hot tub so I don't have to dig through your bag for something for you to sleep in."

She peers over her shoulder at me, and I have to bite the inside of my cheek to keep from making a completely inappropriate sound, watching the steam rise from around her perfect flesh, her tits floating in their lacy confines.

Her natural beauty rips the breath right from my chest.

One of her eyebrows wings up. "You're not going to join me?"

"Um, yeah, I'll be there in a second."

I scramble around, grabbing her clothes from where they're scattered on the floor before I head toward the bathroom to retrieve the laundry bag. Even dusty and sweaty, her shirt and jeans still carry that citrusy scent that's all Athena.

It might be wise to reject her invitation. To climb into the shower and get clean, then pass out on the couch before I can say or do something that might make the rest of our trip awkward somehow. But she wants the company, and as much as I hate to admit it, I've enjoyed our ride today.

Her sass and sense of humor have managed to lighten things that could have thrown other women into fits of hysterics. She's tough as fucking nails, and if she didn't really want me out there with her, she wouldn't have asked.

Twice.

It's all the invitation I need to ignore any reservations and strip down to my boxers, throw all of our clothes into a laundry bag, and grab some cash from my wallet. At these kinds of places, the staff expect to be tipped for doing something like this, and I don't want to be the dick who doesn't slip them some extra cash.

I make my way back and open the door to find the concierge still dutifully waiting.

"Thank you." I extend the laundry bag with a tip toward

him, but the bastard is too busy trying to peer around me to get a look at Athena. "If you want to keep those eyes of yours, I suggest you turn around now."

He jumps, startled as if he just now realized I'm standing here, and he flashes me another smile before he grabs the bag. "Oh, my apologies, sir."

The man practically runs for the elevator across the hall, not daring to look back.

Good.

I wouldn't want to have to throttle him in a five-thousand-dollar-a-night room with Athena Warren right on the other side of the glass. The tabloids would have a field day with that—even if the perv deserved it.

Maybe I deserve a throttling, too, for climbing into that hot tub with her, but she peeks back at me again and waves me in.

Christ, I'm in trouble.

I shut the door and examine the cart of food. They clearly appreciate the Warren family's business enough to want to make a good impression. Can't say I blame them for that. And it means the highest-end items they can offer will be filling our stomachs tonight. I tuck the bottle of champagne under my arm, grab two glasses and the chocolate-covered strawberries, and head for the balcony.

Athena rests in the hot tub, her head thrown back and her eyes closed.

My mouth goes dry, and I struggle to swallow against my equally dry throat. Though it has nothing to do with the fact that we're in the desert.

"Thirsty, Princess?"

I sure as hell am...

Her eyelids flutter open, and those plump lips curl into a smile as she watches me set down everything on the small side table perched by the hot tub. "Mmm, yes, please."

Christ. Why is everything she does so sexy all of a sudden? Does she even know she's doing it?

With Athena, it's hard to tell whether it's intentional or not.

I slip into the hot tub and pop open the champagne. Athena's gaze follows my movements as I pour a glass for each of us. The blue of her eyes seems darker out here, or maybe it's the *way* she's looking at me that makes them seem so different.

Maybe I wasn't the only one who felt that little spark when my arm brushed hers in the elevator.

I hold out one of the glasses for Athena, and she moves closer in the water to take it from my hand. Her soft fingers brush against mine, and another little jolt of something flickers through my fingers and up my arm.

"To great adventures with new friends." I lift my glass.

"Cheers!" She clinks hers against mine and takes a sip, her lips parting to allow it into her mouth.

Shit.

I down my entire glass in one long drink, hoping the cold liquid might cool my libido a little bit.

Athena raises an eyebrow at me. "Bikes? You good?"

Dammit, she's staring at me like I've grown two heads, and no wonder.

I'm lost in my own world, drowning in the blue of her eyes while hot water swirls around her almost-naked body. I clink my empty glass to hers, and she chuckles, reaches for the tray, and grabs a chocolate-covered strawberry.

I should look away because I know what it will likely do to me, but something keeps my eyes locked on her mouth as her lips wrap around the sweet treat.

Visions of where I'd really like to see those lips flash through my head and stir my cock.

Damn. This is going to be a long-ass trip.

CHAPTER 5

ISAIAH

"Oh! My! God!" Athena slides off the bike and breaks into a full run down the sidewalk, leaving me sitting on it until I turn off the engine and slowly slide off with a grin.

The hot tub seems to have helped her soreness. A good meal from room service after, a solid night's sleep, and finally getting her some decent riding gear before we left town didn't hurt, either.

Even though I had planned on waking her up before dawn to get going this morning, when I saw how peaceful she looked sprawled out on the king-sized bed, her dark hair fanned out like a halo against the pillows, I didn't have the heart to wake her.

And I may have stood there and stared at her a little too long, wondering what she was dreaming about.

God knows I spent the night dreaming about what I could see of Athena through the bubbling water in the hot tub. Even though I was a true gentleman and helped her climb out and put on the robe without looking, the few glimpses I got throughout the night were enough to give me very sweet—and frustrating—dreams.

But a little bit of a late start isn't going to mess up our schedule today. Our drive isn't quite as far as yesterday, and we've already made it to Arizona for our mid-day stop. And though we may not be spending as many hours on the bike today, I sure as hell am going to book another room with a hot tub.

For Athena...of course.

Who looks happy as a pig in shit right now, grinning and swinging her arms out as she sings the familiar lyrics at the top of her lungs. She turns to me and points to the sign. "Are we seriously standing on a corner in Winslow, Arizona?"

I chuckle and make my way over to her, joining in her contagious laughter. Something told me she might appreciate my choice of stopping points.

She props one hand on her hip and brings the other to her forehead to shield her eyes from the sun. Her nose scrunches up as she examines me. "You probably have no idea what I'm talking about, do you?"

Fuck, she's cute.

I fight back a grin and point to her. "You're such a fine sight to see."

Athena's mouth hangs open for a moment, then she laughs again. "Oh, my God, you know the Eagles?"

"They're one of my father's favorite bands, and you do realize I'm like ten years older than you are, right? I'm surprised *you* know them."

She scoffs, apparently insulted by the suggestion she might not know a band that recorded that song thirty years before she was even born. "Well, I know you're older, but I wasn't going to *say* anything about it. I didn't want to hurt your feelings. I figured you already knew you're old as fossils."

I bark out another laugh as she playfully bumps her shoulder into mine. "Old as fossils, huh?"

A mischievous grin tilts her lips, and she leans closer. "Practically nothing more than dust in the wind."

"Dust in the wind?" I scowl at her and cross my arms over my chest. "Now you're just showing off with your classic rock knowledge."

She giggles and shakes her head. "My older brothers, Artemis and Archimedes, both really loved classic rock when we were kids. I heard a lot of it growing up—much to the chagrin of my parents who thought it was—and I quote —'wholly inappropriate' noise children shouldn't listen to."

Totally sounds like something the Warrens would say.

I motion toward the statue of Glenn Frey. "Do you want me to take a picture of you standing with Glenn under the sign?"

Athena pulls her phone from her pocket and hands it to me. "Totally. Artie and Archie will flip when they see this. So will my mom."

She wraps her arm around the statue and points to the sign above it that says "STANDIN' ON THE CORNER" and gives me a wide smile that lights up her entire face.

I snap a picture, and she races over and snatches her phone from me, laughing.

Her fingers fly over the screen. "I sent it to Val as proof of life and then to my brothers and mom. Can't wait to see her reaction."

A devious little chuckle slips from her lips, and I lean over to try to read what she wrote.

She pulls away slightly and narrows her eyes on me. "Hey, no peeking."

I take a step back and raise my hands. "Sorry, just wanted

to see what the infamous Bunny Warren had to say about our little stop. I can't imagine she's very happy with you traveling across the country on a motorcycle."

Athena slips her phone into her pocket and shakes her head. "She would be furious, but she doesn't exactly know. I told her I had a ride home but left it at that."

Oh, hell...

I can only imagine the kind of fallout Athena is in for when she gets to New York. Thank God I'll be long gone and on my way back to Boston before the shit hits the fan at the Warren house.

Athena's phone rings in her pocket, and she pulls it out and smiles before answering. "Hey, Artie!...I know, isn't it awesome?" She turns away from me to look at the statue and sign. "I'm *fine.* Don't let Mother's neurosis rub off on you." She nods a few times and scoffs. "I'm not a child, Artie. I'm not going to answer her calls or return them when all she's going to do is scream in my ear about how unacceptable this is. I just want to have some fun."

So, she's been ignoring calls from her mother.

That shouldn't surprise me since I ignored them from *my* family, too, once I made the decision to extend my trip. But it's a little different for Athena. As much as I'm all about equality for the sexes, a twenty-one-year-old girl doing this isn't the same as a thirty-one-year-old man. Any number of horrific things could happen to a woman driving across the country that men rarely have to worry about. I can only imagine how concerned her parents and brothers must be. God knows I would be if she were *my* daughter or little sister.

She taps her foot while she listens to whatever her brother is saying to her. "Tell her and Father and anyone else who asks that I'm being safe. I'll be home in one piece in time for Thanksgiving dinner, and that's all they need to know."

With an exaggerated huff, Athena ends the call and turns back toward me.

"Please tell me you don't try to boss around your brothers the way mine do me."

I chuckle and lead the way toward the diner. "I try not to."

She scowls. "They drive me crazy sometimes."

"They love you, Athena. And that's what big brothers are supposed to do—try to make sure their sisters are safe."

"I guess."

While she says that, the hint of annoyance in her voice tells me that she doesn't always appreciate what her brothers do for her. It's hard to relate when I tend to do the same thing to Jacob and James, at times. But it just comes naturally as part of being the oldest.

I open the door to the diner, and the bell overhead chimes with our arrival.

An older lady behind the counter waves absently toward the tables. "Have a seat anywhere you like, and we'll be with you in a minute."

She's far too busy with the lunch rush to look up or seat us, so we follow her instructions and sit at a table near the window that overlooks the street.

I grab the laminated menus that rest between the napkin holder and the ketchup bottle and hand one to Athena.

Her blue eyes widen, and she licks her lips, scanning the menu. "Oh, I definitely want a cheeseburger and onion rings. What about you? What are you going to get?"

The smile she offers me from over the top of the menu makes me grin back at her.

That shouldn't be so adorable. This girl is too cute for her own good. Or mine.

My phone rings in my pocket, and I pull it out and glance at the screen. Jacob calling—hopefully with an update on the meeting. "Excuse me. I need to take this. Will you just order me the same thing you're having?"

Athena's good mood seems to sour slightly, a slight frown settling on her face.

"Yeah, sure." She waves me off and returns her attention back to the menu.

What was that about?

There isn't any time to get to the bottom of that shift in attitude right now, but I will definitely ask her about it later.

I answer the call as I head out the door. "Hey. What's up?"

"I tried to call you last night, but you didn't answer."

"Yeah, I, uh, didn't have a good signal until now, I guess."

Why am I lying to him?

I had a perfect signal at the Drakeston. I was also having an incredible night, enjoying Athena's company and didn't want to interrupt it by talking to my baby bro.

But he doesn't push me on my failure to answer yesterday.

I lean back against the exterior wall of the diner. "How did the meeting go?"

Jacob scoffs. "*Of course*, it went well. They signed on the dotted line."

"Excellent job, Jacob. I'm really proud of you guys."

"Thanks, Isaiah. We're not totally incompetent, you know." James cuts in over the speakerphone, and I burst out in laughter.

"Who knew these punk kids who used to drive me crazy, trying to tag along with my every step, would wind up being great businessmen?"

"Me. I knew it, you shithead," James shouts, and Jacob laughs at his remark.

Even as annoying as they can sometimes be, I do miss those turds.

I rub a hand over the scruff on my jaw. "Yeah, yeah, I

know. I'm about to grab a bite to eat, so I'll talk to you later, okay?"

Jacob chuckles. "Go eat, be safe, man, talk soon."

I tuck my phone into my pocket and head back inside. Even though I couldn't have been outside more than ten minutes, our food is brought to the table just as I sit down.

Excellent. I'm starving.

"Everything okay?" Athena raises a dark brow at me as I bite into my burger.

I nod and finish chewing. "Yeah, great. It's just a business call."

"Yeah?" Her eyes narrow slightly, like she's trying to unravel some mystery by focusing on me more intently. "Can I ask what your business is?"

The hesitancy in her tone makes me freeze before taking my next bite.

Shit.

Maybe she's figured out I'm not the guy she was supposed to meet up with. That would be bad. It definitely doesn't paint me in a very good light if she finds out I lied about being her ride.

"It's just my family's business."

One of her eyebrows rises slightly. "And you work for them in Boston while going to school in California?"

Shit. Shit. Shit.

I take another bite of my burger to try to buy some time to come up with an answer that sounds believable. "I'm not actually working for the company at the moment." Which is true since I'm technically on vacation. "My brother just had a question about something."

Athena nods slowly, considering my response. It must make sense because she digs back into her plate of food without further comment.

Hell.

Lying to her makes the burger sit heavy in my stomach, but if I tell her I'm not who she thinks I am, this trip will be over. I'm nowhere near ready for that to happen. Not when it's the happiest I've been in as long as I can remember.

ATHENA

Isaiah is lying to me about the call. He shifts uncomfortably on the pleather seat and returns his attention to his food, but my question about the call threw him.

Does he have a girlfriend? Oh my God, he is older. Is he married? What if I'm on a cross-country trip with my crotch plastered to the back of someone's husband?

That would be just my luck—to finally feel a little spark with someone only to find out I'm the *other* woman. The food I just scarfed down makes acid churn in my stomach as we step out of the diner and back into the Arizona sun.

Next time he takes a call, I'll see what I can overhear. Eavesdropping isn't normally my thing since I personally know how annoying it is to have people watching my every move and trying to listen in on private conversations, but I need to know if this man has someone else in his life.

Not because I care for him or like him.

Nope. Definitely not.

I just couldn't live with myself if I found out I was spending all this time with and *flirting with* a married man. The "homewrecker" label isn't one I want to wear. And while this trip is just a shared ride, if I were his significant other, I wouldn't like this at all. A girl on the back of his bike. Sharing a hotel room.

Not cool.

But even if I flat-out asked him, he'd probably just lie to

me like he just did about the "family business." From the looks of his worn-out belongings, Isaiah definitely doesn't look like a man who has any sort of job or family business to support him.

Can I trust anything he says?

"You're awfully quiet." Isaiah bumps my shoulder with his while we walk back toward his bike and offers me a half-smile that doesn't quite reach his eyes.

I don't think we've said two words to each other since he got back from his secret phone call—another thing that raises my hackles. There wasn't any reason for him to get so quiet unless he's hiding something.

"Just thinking."

"Penny for your thoughts?"

Ah, shit.

I can't tell him what I'm thinking. Not only is it none of my business, but he's just a ride home. I shouldn't be prying into his personal life. Even knowing who I am, he hasn't poked me for information about the Warrens the way most people do. He's respected my privacy, and I need to do the same for him.

"Um…" I glance at him out of the corner of my eye, trying to think of a way to divert the conversation away from the awkwardness that seems to have suddenly settled over us. "I was wondering if we could stop at the petrified forest?"

Sounds legit, right?

We will be passing through there, and everything I've ever seen online about it makes it look like a can't-miss stop. Plus, even though my back and ass are feeling a lot better today after the long soak in the hot tub and a good night's sleep in a decent bed, the more breaks we take, the less likely I am to be in agony when we finally stop for the night.

"Yeah, we sure can." Isaiah flashes me a hesitant grin. "Hop on."

The awkward silence that settles over us as we pack our gear and hit the road east makes my chest tighten. Things have been so fun and lighthearted up until now.

What is Mrs. Bikes like?

It's a stupid thing to wonder about—what this man does when he isn't driving strangers across the country. But it floats around my head endlessly while we coast down Route 66.

I bet she's a super-cool chick and likely bikey herself. Isaiah loves his bike and being on the road like this too much to be with a woman who didn't enjoy it. This man definitely isn't into semi-sheltered, totally high-maintenance college chicks.

For some reason, I am not at all ready to explore, that realization makes me swallow back the bile rising up my throat.

Stop obsessing over this, Athena.

It's none of my business, and I need to concentrate on preparing myself to face Mother, Father, Grandfather, and Grandmother at Thanksgiving dinner—likely solo now that I know Bikes has someone in his life. There's no way he's going to want to be my fake date if he has a real *someone* waiting for him in Boston or back in Berkeley.

The road under us changes, and it snaps me from the thoughts that have plagued me since we left the diner. We pass the Painted Desert Visitor Center, and I finally take a good look at our surroundings since I somehow managed to completely miss the fact that we finally arrived at our destination.

Isaiah pulls into a parking spot, and we both climb off the bike and remove our gear—in that same awkward silence that settled over us when we left the diner.

He rubs the back of his neck and motions toward a sign indicating the direction of the trails. "You want to hike?"

I glance out toward the trail. The idea of being alone with him out in the wilderness without the bike and road noise to fill the silences while things are still weird between us doesn't sound appealing at all. "Yeah, not really up for that. I'm still a little tired and sore, and even though I have these much more appropriate boots, I don't want to risk pushing it and feeling like I did last night."

He follows my gaze down to my new boots, and one corner of his mouth lifts into a half-smile. "True. We wouldn't want to push it."

His green eyes stay locked on me, and he shifts his weight and opens his mouth like he wants to say something else. Only he doesn't. All that fun, sexy banter we had last night has disappeared in the wind today, leaving nothing but this uncomfortable tension.

I scan around us, looking for anything to break the silence, and motion toward the building. "Let's go check out the visitor center."

He nods his agreement, and we shuffle along to the entrance—again in tense silence. Isaiah holds the door for me and offers a little smile to me as I step past him.

The gift shop bustles with activity—tourists of all ages examining all the tchotchkes and various souvenirs available. Beautiful, handcrafted art lines the shelves, but the pieces of petrified wood draw me to them.

"You enjoy looking at *wood*, Athena?" Isaiah's voice comes from right next to my ear.

I jump, the whisper of his warm breath against my skin sending tingles all over my body. He snuck up on me so quietly, I hadn't even noticed him. But now, I am *very aware* of how close he stands behind me, heat radiating off his chest and through my back. I elbow him in the ribs playfully.

His responding laugh vibrates through me, sending another shiver down my spine, and he moves off to the left to continue browsing like he didn't just shake me to my core with his comment and my body's reaction.

What the hell was that?

Brushing it off, I snap a pic with a display and shoot a text to Val.

PROOF OF LIFE: LOOKING AT A LOT OF VERY HARD WOOD!

Though it's hard to think of it when things are so…weird between Isaiah and me.

I try to shake it off and keep looking for something for Penelope and Blaire. My sisters-in-law will appreciate the unique items here, and it's never too early to shop for Christmas. I scour the entire shop, but I keep coming back to one particular piece.

The petrified wood jewelry dish whispers silently to something deep inside me. Its beauty almost bringing tears to my eyes.

"Hello, young lady. May I help you?" The older man behind the counter offers me a kind smile.

For some reason, he reminds me of Grandfather, only less stern. It reminds me that I'm going to have to face the old man in only a few days. Even with Grandmother as a buffer, he's sure to tear into me about my plans for after graduation, just like he has every single time we've seen each other since I started college almost four years ago.

And I'll give him the same answer I always do—I don't know yet.

That isn't totally true, but it's better than giving him the honest answer and starting an argument we don't need at the family table.

I smile at the old man and point to the jewelry dish in the display case. "Hi. I'll take this piece, please."

"Oh, I'm sorry, but that's been sold. Anything else catching your eye?"

"Oh." My heart sinks slightly, and I stare at it longingly, a strange sense of loss settling over me. "Okay. No, thank you."

He takes the piece from the display and wraps it up, and I spend a few more minutes in the gift shop, looking for anything else that might catch my eye. But nothing draws me in the way that piece did.

Bummer.

I pay for the things I picked for Penelope and Blaire and scan the store but can't find Isaiah anywhere, so I head outside to see if he's by the bike. His back is toward me as he looks out over the painted desert. Of course, he's out here on his phone, but my boots must give away my approach because he glances over his shoulder at me.

"I'll call you tomorrow." He ends the call and stuffs his phone into his pocket.

"Everything okay?" I try to sound casual with the question, but what I really want to ask sits on the tip of my tongue.

Who were you talking to? Your wife?

"Yeah, just another call from the family." He shrugs nonchalantly, but the tension in his shoulders gives away the fact that the call was a lot more than that. He peeks down at my bag. "You get some souvenirs?"

Way to change the subject...

I could call him out on the fact that I think he's lying, but I don't want the rest of this trip to be filled with weirdness between us. "The piece I really liked was already sold, but I got a couple of things for my sisters-in-law."

That should be the end of it. I should climb onto the bike and just let it go, but this time, I can't bite back the question.

"You didn't find anything? Nothing for Mrs. Bikes or potentially future Mrs. Bikes?" I bite the inside of my cheek as I wait for his answer.

It shouldn't matter, right?

He's an adult and can make his own life decisions when they don't affect me in any way.

No, it doesn't matter. It absolutely doesn't matter.

I just need to know for curiosity's sake. That's all.

Yeah, right, Athena.

"Mrs. Bikes?" Isaiah's dark eyebrows wing up, and he laughs, practically doubling over.

The sound floating through the air to me and the way his face lights up with his laughter makes the man even sexier.

So damn sexy.

When he finally regains control of himself, he grabs my helmet off the handlebars and hands it to me. "There isn't a Mrs. Bikes, Athena. Do you really think I would have climbed into that hot tub with you last night if there were?"

"Well...I—"

He leans closer to me. "You thought I was some asshole who would get almost naked with another girl when I was married?"

Crap. That does sound bad.

"I'm sorry. I just..."

"You just what?"

I sigh and wave a dismissive hand in his direction. "Nothing. Forget it. I'm sorry it seemed like I thought you were a total asshole about that."

He grins at me, and warmth floods my entire body at the humor dancing in his green eyes. "So, you don't think I'm a total asshole?"

"Oh, you're an asshole. Just not because of that. You *did* laugh at me when I was pissing on the side of the road."

He barks out a laugh and grabs his helmet. "Fair enough. We're headed to Albuquerque now, or was there somewhere else you wanted to stop?"

"Is it far?" I slip on my helmet and fasten it without a

struggle this time. I'm getting much more proficient with this gear.

"It's just a couple of hours from here. We'll be able to get a decent night's rest."

"Yeah, sounds good."

Isaiah pulls on his helmet with that same ease he naturally seems to have, and I can't help the way my eyes follow his every move. Now that I know he isn't married, there isn't any guilt over watching him turn to grab his gloves, giving me the perfect view of his backside.

"Athena? Everything okay?"

Shit, did he just bust me checking him out? God, how embarrassing.

I jerk my focus from his ass to the playful glint in his eyes. "Yeah, why wouldn't it be?"

He grins at me. Clearly, he didn't miss my perusal of his derriere. "I don't know." He shrugs. "You just seem a bit off since lunch at the diner."

Because I thought you were married.

No way I am admitting that to Isaiah, though. The last thing I need him doing is giving me the third degree about why I care when I don't even know the answer to that.

CHAPTER 6

ATHENA

The front desk clerk offers me an apologetic smile. "Sorry, miss, we only have one room available for this evening."

Seriously?

It's like the universe is conspiring against me to force me to sleep in the same room with this gorgeous man. Isaiah might be the perfect roommate when it comes to cleanliness and manners, but I need a break from his hotness.

I literally bear hug him all day with my entire body, with my vagina pressed against his back, and now, I have to stay in the same room with him—again.

Just freaking great.

At least I know he isn't married, but he never *did* say whether or not there was a potential future Mrs. Bikes out there. Not married doesn't mean not seriously involved. I would hope he wouldn't be flirting with me so much if he has a girlfriend, but who knows with some men.

"That'll be fine." Isaiah smiles at the clerk. "We'll take it."

He slides his card across the counter to pay, but I put my hand on his to stop it from reaching the attendant. The warmth of his skin against my palm makes my breath hitch for a second, and he turns toward me slightly to argue.

I hold up my free hand to silence him before he starts. "Seriously, I have it, Isaiah. I told you, it's the least I can do since I can't help you drive. Let me get it."

He casts a quick glance at the clerk, who keeps his head down and pretends to be typing something even though I'm quite confident he's faking it and just trying to give us a little privacy for our little spat. "I'm not broke, Athena. I can help pay for things."

Oh, God, I'm being too obvious about his lack of money.

I've hurt his feelings and probably embarrassed him by offering to pay in front of this guy. In just over six months, immediately after graduation, I'll be in his shoes and know how it feels. But now, I'm apparently oblivious and feel like a real asshole for insisting I pay over and over again. I should just let Isaiah takes care of the room tonight so his pride remains intact.

"Sure." I offer him a smile I hope doesn't give away how uncomfortable this whole thing makes me. "I didn't think you were. Please go ahead and thank you."

I grab my bags and hustle away from the front desk as fast as my slightly achy ass and tired legs can carry me. The last place I want to be if his card gets declined is standing next to him. It'll just embarrass him and make everything more awkward.

Lord knows I don't need any more of that.

It's the perfect time to check in with Valerie. I take a selfie with the hotel lobby in the background. This isn't The Drakeston—far from it, actually—but it isn't bad. No bad smells. Clean appearance. Relatively busy.

I fire off a text to Valerie with the photo.

PROOF OF LIFE: ATE A GAS STATION HOTDOG. ARRIVED IN ALBUQUERQUE.

Isaiah joins me a few moments later. "All set."

He reaches out and takes my bag from my hand. I let him have it without a fight. Isaiah seems to be almost as set in his ways as I am, and he appears to think it's his duty as a gentleman to carry everything.

"We're on the second floor." He glances over at me with a lopsided grin. "Wonder if we'll be sharing rooms this entire trip?"

His joke breaks a bit of the tension between us, but I can't help but wonder about that very thing.

"Right?"

What are the chances the two hotels we chose are almost fully booked?

I laugh, and it releases a little of the tightness in my chest that the thought of spending another night in a room alone with Isaiah has brought.

Things aren't like that between us. I just need to keep reminding myself of that. He may be gorgeous. I would have to be blind not to notice that, but he's not my boyfriend, and this isn't some kind of date. He's just giving me a ride home for Thanksgiving. Nothing more.

I need to chill out on the guilt and all these weird feelings I'm letting this situation bring up. Absolutely nothing untoward has happened. If anything, we've just become friends.

Friends who share champagne and chocolate-covered strawberries while almost naked in a hot tub...

I take a deep, cleansing breath and follow him over to the elevator. He reaches forward to press the call button, and I force myself to keep my focus on the shiny doors in front of us instead of letting my gaze drift down to his butt again.

What is it about this guy's ass in jeans?

I swear to God, it's like a magnet wants to drag my eyes

right down there, but the immediate ding of the doors sliding open for us saves me from the inevitable failure of my willpower.

He motions for me to enter in front of him, and he joins me inside the cab, presses the button for the floor, and settles next to me. "You sure you don't want anything else to eat or drink?"

"No, I'm still full. Who knew a gas station hotdog could be so delicious?"

Seriously, not me.

Isaiah chuckles and points to himself. "Me. I love a good gas station hotdog."

"Well, Bunny Warren would *never* stop at a gas station for food, even if her life depended on it. The woman would rather starve than subject herself or her children to anything that can be bought from a cashier."

He laughs and shakes his head. "Why does that not surprise me?"

I shrug, and the elevator dings and comes to a stop. "She doesn't know what she's missing out on. That might have been the best hot dog I've ever eaten in my life."

Isaiah smirks as he steps out into the hallway. "And it didn't have anything to do with the fact that it was the first thing you had eaten since lunch and you were starving?"

Following him down to our room, I laugh and consider his question. "I mean, *maybe*. Or maybe it was just *that* good."

He shrugs and slips the key into the door. "Maybe both?"

I grin at him. "Maybe."

It might be stupid and childish, but I cross my fingers for a double bed situation. I scrambled away from the front desk before they could give us any specifics about the one remaining room.

Isaiah ushers me inside ahead of him, and I step in and come face to face with one bed.

I sigh and drop my purse onto the small console where the TV sits. "This is so strange, like we're cursed with only having one hotel room available."

A low, deep chuckle comes from behind me, sending a little shiver over me. "At least you know I'm not a total pervert. I haven't attacked you yet."

I turn back toward him and raise an eyebrow with a laugh. "Yet?"

He grins and waggles his eyebrows at me suggestively. "I saw how you were looking at that wood today."

"Perv!" I toss my water bottle at him. "Hey! You better stop!"

"You looked pretty upset that you didn't get the piece of wood you wanted." He grabs the hem of his shirt, pulls it off and over his head, and tosses it into his bag on the floor. "Is that why you've been quiet since then?"

"Huh?"

Suddenly, I've forgotten how to speak. The only things that exist in this world are those abs and that *V* thirst-trap thing that's making me stupid. I only caught a glimpse of it last night since I had my eyes closed in the hot tub when he slipped in and climbed out. But they are *wide* open now.

Stop looking at his abs, Athena. Stop looking at his abs.

"Princess, you keep looking at me like that, and it's going to be a different kind of wood we're talking about."

Unwillingly—so damn unwillingly—I force my eyes from his masterpiece torso and shift my focus up to his face.

The fire that blazes across his green gaze sends a shudder of anticipation down my spine.

Good God!

No man has ever looked at me like that—with the barely restrained hunger.

And I am *sooo* out of my element here.

A nervous laugh bubbles from my lips, and I grab my bag

and head straight to the bathroom, not stopping until there's a locked door between us.

How the hell am I supposed to spend the night alone in a room with a man who looks like that...who looks at me like that...and not think about touching him?

ISAIAH

"Princess, you keep looking at me like that, and it's going to be a different kind of wood we're talking about."

Her eyes shift up to my face and grow to the size of saucers. The normally ocean-blue darkens to an almost navy, but her shock at my words makes her practically shake.

Shit.

That was totally out of line, but it just slipped right out of my mouth before I could stop it. Like my filter just disappeared for a split-second. Sometimes I forget I've only known this girl for a few days. Comments I would normally only make with Jacob and James, one of my buddies, or with a girl I had been friends with or had been dating for a long time just seem so natural.

Things with Athena have just gotten so comfortable—like we've known each other our entire lives rather than spent most of our time together in silence on the road.

It shouldn't excuse what I said, though.

I open my mouth to apologize and offer to go sleep in the lobby or find somewhere to camp after my verbal diarrhea, but she bursts out laughing, the sound sharp and making me jump slightly. Athena shakes her head, grabs her bag, and races to the bathroom without another word.

Damn. She laughed at me?

In all the years I've been pursuing women—basically,

since I hit high school—I'm pretty sure I've never been laughed at like that. Not by *any* girl. If anything, I'm usually the ones rejecting them—though, I've never stooped low enough to actually *laughing* at a woman who shows interest in me. Even I'm not *that* cruel.

Talk about a blow to the ego.

That one actually hurts, and I reach up and rub at the ache that has suddenly formed in my chest. But her laughing is better than her being pissed or frightened. The last thing I would ever want to do is make Athena feel that she's not safe with me. This entire crazy road trip happened because I wanted to ensure she didn't fall prey to that perverted asshole she was supposed to ride with—or anyone else along the way.

And now, I let our friendly banter and flirting go too far.

Dumbass move, Isaiah.

I move across the room to the windows that offer a view of the mountains surrounding Albuquerque. It really is beautiful, what I can see of it in the dark anyway. Tiny lights dot the landscape, likely farms and houses spaced out across the desert where people get to enjoy the mountains and fresh air. But as pretty as the desert might be, my mind keeps drifting back to a different pretty thing, and she's in the bathroom, taking a shower—and avoiding me.

Scrubbing my hands over my face, I release a frustrated groan.

Dammit.

I'm two days into this trip, and this woman is starting to crawl under my skin. And it's not just because she has her arms wrapped around me and her body pressed to mine for hours and hours every day. It isn't just because she's a stunning, classic beauty who belongs on a cover of a magazine— not simply for being a Warren.

It's the way her laughter is infectious and her sense of

humor always makes me smile. Her strength and determination not to let this trip and what it's doing to her physically break her. Her intelligence and worldly view despite the fact that the way she was raised sheltered her from so many things that are just part of other people's everyday lives—like gas station hotdogs.

But none of that matters. It can't. Athena would never be interested in an older man who spends all his time working. She's young, vibrant, and hell, she's still in college. She hasn't even had time to experience life outside of school yet. It took me a long time to figure out who I was and what I wanted out of life once I graduated. Despite the spark and connection we clearly share, I need to keep this arrangement exactly what it was in the beginning—me driving her home to ensure she arrives safely.

That's all that it *can* be.

My phone vibrates in my pocket, but I ignore it and keep staring out at the city. If it's anything important, whoever it is will leave a message I can listen to later. Right now, I need to try to figure out a way to ignore my attraction to Athena so I can get back into the "friend zone" with her before I say something else to make her uncomfortable.

I don't know how long I stay in this position, blankly looking out at the flickering lights, but Athena eventually emerges from the bathroom, the sound of the door opening making me turn back to face the room.

She steps out in a long T-shirt that hits her mid-thigh, with her dark, wet hair hanging around her face and fresh, make-up-free face flawless in the moonlight streaming in from the windows.

Hell.

The woman is even more beautiful like this than she is in her skin-tight jeans and all made up.

"You finished in there?" My tone comes off harsher than I

intended, but it seems when she's around me, I don't really have any ability to keep my cool.

I should apologize for how it sounded. It's not her fault that I find her beautiful, intelligent, and charming. I just need to figure out a way to deal with these feelings without making her think she did anything wrong.

She swallows thickly and motions toward the bathroom. "Yeah, go ahead. I'll just take a pillow and blanket and sleep on the floor. You can have the bed since you paid for the room."

I scan the room and really take in everything for the first time since we entered. There isn't even a couch or a chair. Definitely a step down from the Drakeston honeymoon suite, but it wasn't like we had a lot of choices rolling into town without a reservation.

Shaking my head, I close the distance between us and stop in front of her until I'm close enough for the crisp scent of her soap and light, citrusy smell of her shampoo to invade my breath. "Absolutely not. I'll sleep on the floor. You'll be sleeping in the bed, Princess."

Does she really think I'd let her sleep on the floor? What type of assholes has she been dating?

"Isaiah, you paid for this room. Plus, I had the benefit of a high-end mattress last night in Vegas. It's only fair that—"

"Princess." I hold up my hand to silence whatever argument she's about to put up against this. "Just get in the bed. Please."

I'm not sure I have the strength in me tonight to get into a disagreement with Athena over something as stupid as where she's sleeping.

She huffs, but whatever retort she was about to give dies on her tongue. Her blue eyes meet mine, and she quickly looks away and toward the bed. "You know, we could just both sleep in it." She shrugs as she moves to the source of our disagreement to turn down the covers. "We're both adults, after all. What's the problem?"

Oh, I only see one problem with that.

I'm headed to take a cold shower to cope with it.

The thought of sleeping next to her, of her brushing up against me, or worse…wanting to cuddle, is almost too much to comprehend.

But if she's cool with it, then I guess I should be, too.

I can do this.

I'm not some animal incapable of controlling my desires and urges. I wasn't even when I was in college. Respect for women has been ingrained in me since the day I was born.

I can totally sleep next to this intelligent, funny, beautiful woman and keep it all business.

No problem at all.

"Hop in bed, Athena. I'm going to shower."

Maybe twice.

This is going to be a long night.

CHAPTER 7

ATHENA

L ast night was hell.
At least, it was for me.

Every time Isaiah shifted in the slightest, my body tensed, hyper-aware of his presence and anticipating his next move. Warm breath fluttered against my skin too many times to count. Mumbled words left me struggling to decipher them. His fingers brushed against mine in his sleep, and heat flooded every one of my limbs until I felt like I was going to combust just from that slight touch.

Imagine what his full attention focused solely on me would feel like.

I squirm against the leather seat at the thought, instinctively rubbing my open legs against Isaiah's jean-clad ass.

No, don't imagine that, Athena.

DO. NOT. IMAGINE. THAT.

I would love to say this is all because I've never slept in the same bed as a man before. That it is just a new experience that left me on edge and uncertain.

But that isn't it. That isn't *only* it.

It's because it was *him.* Because Isaiah has managed to work his way past the defenses I typically put up around guys to protect myself from those who may want a shot at the only female Warren heir.

He isn't just handsome. He's kind and really fun, and he is genuinely nice—except for the whole laughing-at-me-while-I-peed-in-the-desert thing. He definitely isn't like most guys who try to spend time with me—a frat boy out for himself and a good time.

Even now, as we make our way toward Amarillo, I can't help but laugh at the one place he said he wanted to stop—the Big Texan Steak Ranch. Isaiah is dying to try their seventy-two-ounce steak challenge.

It sounds like a whole lot of indigestion to me, but the man says he loves his steak, so I'm happy to cheer him on and watch him make an attempt.

We pull into the parking lot, and a huge, bright-yellow building looms before us. Isaiah shuts off the engine, and I inhale deeply. The smell wafting out from inside makes my stomach growl in an incredibly unladylike way. It's been hours since we ate lunch, but I hadn't realized just how hungry I really was until this moment.

Isaiah chuckles and looks over his shoulder at me. "You ready to eat?"

I nod enthusiastically. "Starving."

One of his eyebrows wings up, and he gives a little smirk. "You going to try the seventy-two-ounce steak challenge, Princess?"

Isaiah laughs like it's the funniest thing he's ever heard while I slide off the motorcycle. The man clearly doesn't understand how much a woman can eat when she's motivated by beating him.

"Oh, you bet your ass I'm going to. I'm going to mop the

floor with you, *Bikes*."

Humor glints in his green gaze. "You're talking a bunch of shit, Princess. You care to make a bet?"

He climbs off the bike and turns to me.

I don't even hesitate, facing him with a determined, steely gaze. "I absolutely want to make a bet."

A bet that might get me what I really want...

It's time to unleash the idea that's been brewing in my mind since the first time I laid eyes on Isaiah a few days ago at Whiskey Jack's.

"If I win, you have to spend Thanksgiving weekend with me at my family's house and pretend to be my boyfriend."

Isaiah's eyes darken slightly, and he tilts his head as if he's studying me and can't figure me out. "Why in the world would you want to do that? They'll flip out if I roll up with their little princess on the back of a Harley."

I don't bother fighting the grin that pulls at my lips. "Exactly." I poke him square in his hard chest. "My parents are always meddling, and this way, I can ensure that I can actually enjoy the holiday without them trying to set me up."

Goodbye Cliff Clifton.

"Do we have a deal?" I extend my hand and wait.

"Ah, ah, ah, not so fast." Isaiah shakes his head and offers a sly grin. "You haven't heard *my* terms."

It doesn't matter what his terms are…unless it's sleeping with him, and I'd almost consider it to avoid any set-ups from my parents. Almost.

"What are your terms?"

He points at me. "You promise not to get mad when I beat you like a rug in here. We got a deal?"

That's all he wants?

Isaiah extends his hand, but before we can shake, his phone rings. He looks annoyed and grabs it from his pocket.

After a quick glance at the screen, he silences it and stuffs the phone back in his pocket.

Nope. Not suspicious at all.

He may say he's not married, but something is definitely going on that Isaiah doesn't want me to know about. Maybe I should have added that he has to truthfully answer twenty questions when I win.

But it's too late to change the terms now. He holds out his hand again, and we shake, his much larger palm wrapping around mine tightly. Only, he doesn't let go. Instead, Isaiah uses our entangled hands to propel me in front of him.

He whips me around like I'm light as a feather. "Come on, Princess. Time to tie on the old feed bag."

Yeehaw. I have a bet to win!

We enter the fray, and a cacophony of sound and smells bombard us. My mouth waters as I watch a waiter roll a steak by on a tray.

Isaiah has no idea I'm about to beat his pants off.

Crap. Crap. Crap. Wrong thing to think.

Now an image of Isaiah, pantsless, standing in the middle of the dining room, bombards my mind.

The giggle rips from between my lips before I can stop it.

Isaiah narrows his eyes on me. "What? What are you laughing at, Athena? What's so funny?"

I can't help it. My laughter only increases, bordering on hysterics. Maybe I should have included his pants in this bet. I try to wave him off, but I keep doubling over with my fits of hysteria. "Nothing, Bikes. Nothing at all. Just thinking about something."

He cocks one brow at me.

Shit, that's hot as hell.

I'm not surprised, though. Everything he does is sexy. The man is literally walking sex in tight jeans and a beat-up leather jacket. And I am *soooo* here for it.

A playful grin tugs at the corners of his lips. "I don't trust you one bit, Princess." He grabs me, turns me so my back is tight against his chest, and wraps his arms around me in a cocoon, using his hands to lock me in place. "You're staying here so I can keep an eye on you."

Oh, my damn.

I swoon so hard that my legs might actually collapse right out from under me if Isaiah weren't holding me so tightly against his chest. His delicious scent—leather and road and all man—envelops me and makes my mouth water more than any smell in this damn restaurant can. Warm and firm behind me, I fight the urge to rub myself all over him.

My God, this man!

It's like nothing in this world can bother me with him at my back. And I like this feeling—a lot.

Way too much.

"Two?" a gum-popping hostess asks.

"Yes." Isaiah rests his chin on top of my head.

The gesture is so casual, so natural, that I can't help but release a little sigh. As pathetic as it might make me, it comes out all the same.

The hostess grabs a couple of menus, and Isaiah begins moving me forward, his arms wrapped tightly around me.

No one could wipe this smile off my face, no matter how hard they tried. Nothing could, not even Mother or Father or Grandfather could ruin this for me right now.

Being in his arms feels right. Too right.

What the hell does that even mean?

The hostess stops in front of a booth, and Isaiah releases me so I can slide into one side. I wait for him to move and sit across from me, but instead, he taps my thigh.

"Scoot over, Princess."

What? He wants to sit beside me?

I don't bother fighting a smile and scoot over to give him

enough room to sit next to me. The hostess hands us the menus, and I can't focus on anything other than the fact that Isaiah's rock-hard, muscled thigh presses against mine.

Shit. I need to focus. I have a bet to win.

ISAIAH

The moment I wrapped my arms around Athena, every problem and stress in my life seemed to vanish. I forgot about what waits for me back in Boston, about who just called while we were out in the parking lot, and what the potential reasons for the call might have been. It just felt... right to have her in my arms. The same way it does when *she's* wrapped around *me* on that bike for hours at a time.

And now that she's slipped from my grip and settled into the booth, I don't want to take the other side and be so far away from her.

Christ, that sounds stupid.

It's a damn booth. No more than two feet can separate us if I slide onto the opposite bench. But something compels me to nudge her thigh all the same.

She glances up at me with warm blue eyes.

"Scoot over, Princess."

A tiny grin plays at her perfect lips, and she shifts to let me slip in next to her. I press my leg against hers, ensuring our bodies touch even when the hostess hands us the menus.

I dip my head and pretend to examine the menu even though we both already know that we're doing the challenge. Athena shifts next to me, pressing her thigh against mine a little harder even though there's plenty of room on the other side of her on the bench.

Fighting a grin, I lower my hand to her thigh and

squeeze. She freezes for a second, her flesh under my palm going hard and tight, then she angles herself even more toward me.

I shift my hand higher.

Slowly.

Oh, so damn slowly.

"Hey, guys! I'm Wendy!" She slides two glasses of water onto the table in front of us and offers a smile. "What can I get for y'all?"

Perfect damn timing!

I reluctantly pull my hand from Athena's leg and point to the menu where the challenge is outlined. "We'll both be doing the challenge. Medium rare."

Wendy's eyes bulge, examining Athena sitting next to me. "She wants to do the challenge?"

Athena leans forward slightly so Wendy can see her fully. "I'm going to kick his ass."

Our waitress stands stunned silent for a moment, then lets out a laugh that draws the attention of everyone at all the tables around ours. "Oh, honey. I would *pay* to see that. Two medium rare challenge steaks coming up!"

"And a couple IPAs."

There is no way I'm eating a massive steak without some beer to wash it down.

As soon as she walks back toward the kitchen, I turn to Athena and squeeze her thigh again. "You scared our poor waitress."

She drops her jaw in mock indignation. "I did *not*!"

"Did so."

Her laughter tickles my hair, and she leans in and brushes her lips against my ear. "Maybe I enjoy keeping people on their toes."

I chuckle and shake my head, reaching out to take a long sip of the ice-cold water at the table to quell the scorching heat rising in my blood. "Oh, I have no doubt you do, Princess."

Our waitress returns and points to a huge table that runs along the front of the restaurant's dining room. "Challengers eat up there."

Shit.

I hadn't planned on an audience, but it doesn't seem to faze Athena at all. She nudges my leg to get me to scoot out of the booth and lets me follow her up onto the raised dais and to our seats at the table.

In record time, the waitress sets two massive plates with the biggest steaks I've ever seen in my life in front of us. She chuckles and then lowers two shrimp cocktails, baked potatoes, salads, and rolls with butter to the table, too. "Good luck, guys."

The scent of beef wafts up into my face. It smells delicious, but shit, this is a lot of food.

"You ready to get your ass kicked, Bikes?" Athena pulls her hair back and ties it up out of the way.

"Damn, you're taking this very seriously, Princess. But I guess you should. A tiny thing like you, no way you're going to out-eat me." I laugh and pat my stomach.

She's a buck and a quarter at most. I've got a good hundred pounds on her. Yet, she doesn't seem concerned in the least.

That should probably concern me, shouldn't it?

"What you don't know, Isaiah..." She pauses and furrows her brow.

Hell, I guess I never told her my last name.

This girl is entirely too fucking trusting. That's precisely the reason I'm driving her home. Not that fact that she's beautiful or that she keeps rubbing her thigh against mine in the best, distracted way.

"Wolfe."

"What you don't know, Isaiah Wolfe, is that growing up with two older brothers, if I wanted anything, I had to fight for it. I don't lose, Bikes. I don't fucking lose. Ever."

Her confidence is sexy as hell, and I can see Athena doesn't back down from a challenge. I like that about her. Just one more thing to add to the already-long list.

"Okay, Princess, may the best man win, and before you tell me how sexist that is, I said man because *I* will win." I offer her my biggest smile.

But she isn't finding me cute right now. Athena is all business.

"Shut up and focus on your meat." Somehow, she manages to keep a straight face while saying that, but I can't help the laugh that spills from my lips.

She points her fork at me and raises one eyebrow. I just laugh harder in response.

The waitress asks if we want to take a test bite of our steaks before we begin the challenge, but I wave her off and start cutting the massive piece of meat. Once Athena and I both have our steaks cut and ready, the timer starts.

Everyone claps and cheers, and Athena wastes no time digging in. I begin with the humongous steak, my mind already protesting what my stomach is about to attempt.

There isn't any way Athena is eating all of this. I'm not even sure I can get it all down, but one thing I *never* have been is a quitter. With one hour on the clock, I'm giving it my best shot. Especially because I don't want to lose to Athena.

But really, even if I lose, I'm still kind of winning.

Aren't I?

Knowing what little I do about the Warrens and the drama that's been happening in the family the last two years, I can understand why Athena might want to stick it to her parents. Their dynamic must be all kinds of messed up. She wants someone there to help her get through the holiday, and something deep inside me wants *me* to be that person.

For a split second, I consider eating a little slower. But Athena would *literally* kick my ass if I didn't try my best to beat her. So, it's chow time.

We both tuck into our dinners, and I do as Athena ordered and focus on my meat.

CHAPTER 8

ATHENA

I should *not* have eaten that whole thing.
What the hell was I thinking?
WIN!

I had been so intent on kicking Isaiah's ass that I didn't even care that it might mean I would be miserable later.

And God knows I am.

Climbing onto the back of that metal horse and riding for hours until we reached Oklahoma City after eating the equivalent of a full family meal might have been my penance for every bad thing I've ever done in my entire twenty-one years on this planet.

But I won.

Which means my co-conspirator will be at my side all of Thanksgiving dinner and weekend, helping me convince Mother to back off from her matchmaking plans with Cliff Clifton and maybe, just maybe, pissing her off enough to have her stop altogether.

That is worth every miserable moment of this agony.

I should have just made myself throw up as soon as we made it out of there. Getting all this out of my stomach might have helped, but it tasted so good that I didn't want to let it go to waste. Plus, yacking would have undermined my win.

It wouldn't be nearly as bad if Isaiah were suffering with me, but while I'm lying on this hotel bed in agony, stuffed so full that it literally feels like my stomach might rupture, *that* asshole is as fresh as a damn daisy, still light on his feet with that cocky grin on his face even though he lost. He was even gracious about that, though. Now I am starting to think that had more to do with the fact that he anticipated the discomfort I would be in for trying to prove I could beat his ass.

The lock to the room clicks.

Speak of the devil.

And to add insult to injury, I had to send him to the store for me on a "necessity" run. I'm far too near death's door to get back on that bike tonight.

Isaiah saunters in with two plastic bags hanging from his hand, his steps still as light and effortless as if he hadn't consumed just as much food as I did only a few hours ago. "Okay, Athena. I got you some antacids, ginger ale, water, and some crackers."

The thought of crackers makes me gag and bury my face in the pillow again.

Yuck.

"Ughh. Thank you, but I don't want to think about anything that even remotely looks like food ever again, much less eat it."

I consumed enough calories today to live off for at least a week, maybe more, but I just need to keep reminding myself of my victory. Isaiah wasn't even able to *finish* his steak and pushed away his plate with at least a third of it still sitting there. Even knowing how much he had eaten—because even without finishing that monster, it was still *a lot* of food—I made sure he knew how lame I thought he was for letting a woman half his size show him up.

He issues a low chuckle and sets the bags on the bed. "You will have to eat again at *some* point, Princess."

Releasing a groan, I shift to try to sit up to at least take the antacids that might quell some of the gurgling lava in my stomach, but Isaiah grabs me with his strong hands before I can blink or even make it up onto my elbow.

He settles on the edge of the bed and grabs me to help me sit up. "Wait, Princess. Let me help you for the sake of my conscience."

I turn my head to examine his creased brow and concerned green eyes. "Your conscience?"

He sighs and squeezes my shoulder gently. "It's my fault you're in this situation. I wanted to go do the challenge."

Yeah, but I didn't have to challenge *him to the challenge. That was all me.*

Artie always said that sometimes I push too hard and move too fast, and this would definitely be one of those times. Even Grandmother, who has tried to be more supportive recently, has warned me to slow down before I burn myself out.

Right now, I'm not burning; I'm about to explode.

Oh, God. I'm going to puke.

Somehow, I suddenly manage to move faster than I thought possible in my current engorged state.

I slide by Isaiah and race toward the bathroom as fast as my sore legs can carry me, with my hand over my mouth. That delicious, juicy steak is about to make a reappearance in a very not pretty way.

But I don't have time to care about anything, not how I look or what unflattering things Isaiah may hear. All my focus needs to be on throwing up the lid to the toilet fast enough and heaving my guts out.

Oh, God. Oh, God.

My head swims and my stomach turns, presenting its contents as an offering to the porcelain god.

Over. And over. And over again.

Isaiah's heavy, booted footsteps thunk on the tile as he crosses it toward me. He squats next to me and rubs a hand down my back slowly. The touch that should just be comforting also sends a jolt of reality back into my foggy mind.

He just watched me puke. Lovely.

"I'm so sorry." I flush the toilet, then scoot away from it— and him—to rest my back against the wall and close my eyes.

The coolness of tiles at my back seeps into my warm skin, helping quell the need to heave—at least somewhat. Though, they can't do anything about the embarrassment clenching my stomach. I'm sure I'm a real vision, and I must smell like absolute shit right now.

Isaiah pushes to his feet, and the movement and curiosity over what he's doing pull open my eyelids.

He offers me a little half-smile. "There's nothing to apologize for, Princess."

Yeah, right.

I have a lot of things to apologize for—the least of which is retching in front of him. If I hadn't wanted to avoid another setup and drive Mother and Father batshit crazy, I never would have even considered coming home any other way than the jet. I never would have jumped on the back of a stranger's bike. I never would have flirted with him and become so competitive with him.

He grabs a washcloth and wets it under the faucet.

Oh, God, no.

My stomach turns again, and I push myself up just in time to make it back to the toilet.

If the Earth could open up and swallow me whole right now so I never have to look this gorgeous man in the eye again, that would be just great.

ISAIAH

Athena retches again, for what feels like the hundredth time. If this feels never-ending to me, I can't even imagine how awful she must feel. And from the looks of it, she feels pretty fucking awful.

Hair wet and plastered to her face and neck by sweat. Cheeks red yet somehow pale at the same time. Tiny whimpers slipping from the lips I want to kiss so badly.

I'd be more concerned if I knew it wasn't from the massive amount of food she just ate. She just needed to get it out. It was really too much—even for me. The tiny girl must have an iron stomach to have kept it down this long with the hours we spent on the road from Amarillo to Oklahoma City.

But she beat me, fair and square. And as much as I hate seeing her so miserable, pride also swells in my chest that she actually did it. The woman just gets more and more impressive the longer I spend with her.

Athena hangs her head, resting it on one of her arms that's draped across the rim of the toilet. Seeing her like this makes my chest ache.

Anything I can do to help her, I will at least try.

I duck out of the bathroom to pour a glass of ginger ale for her. It isn't much, but it may calm her stomach a bit.

She hasn't moved an inch when I return with it.

"Here, take a sip of this." I hold out the glass.

It takes her a moment to drag up her head from her arm to see what I have. Cloudy blue eyes attempt to focus on it, then she closes them and shakes her head slightly before reopening them and finally managing to see what I'm holding.

She accepts it with a shaking hand, takes a small sip, and offers it back to me. "Kill me. Kill me now. If I ever see food again, it will be too soon."

Vague memories of horrible late nights and mornings on the bathroom floor of my college apartment come flooding back. Even though it's been a decade since I ended my partying days, I can still remember what it felt like to be so miserable that I would say I would never drink again.

It always changed the moment I felt better, and by tomorrow morning, Athena will be back to her old self and scarfing down some greasy diner food with me on the road.

It doesn't do much to help her now, though.

I move in and sweep her sweat-dampened hair from her neck.

She lamely tries to shoo me away with a flailing arm. "I'm so gross. You don't want to touch me."

"You're not gross, Athena." I scoop up her hair, move it away from her face, and hold it back.

Far from it.

"I think I'm gonna be sick again."

"Go ahead, Princess. I've got you."

I reach over to the bathroom counter and grab a hair tie from her overnight bag. Gently brushing my fingers through the dark strands, I pull her hair back into a ponytail and secure it as she retches again. "Is that better?"

She finally stops this round of misery and sucks in a deep breath, letting her eyes flutter closed. "Thank you, Bikes."

"I'd do anything to help you feel better, Princess."

Even though it feels woefully inadequate in this moment. Watching someone you care about go through hell is about the worst feeling in the world.

And as much as I may not want to fully admit it, I do care about Athena. Far more than I should when I've only known her a few days. Far more than I should when this entire thing is based on a lie—even one designed to protect her.

Athena leans back against the tiled wall again and takes another sip of the ginger ale before releasing a heavy breath.

"Do you think you're done?"

She nods slightly, her eyes still closed.

"Come on, Princess." I scoop her up from the floor, and she wraps her arms around my neck and buries her face against my cheek. "Let's get you tucked in."

We have another long day ahead of us tomorrow, and if we're going to make it to New York by Thanksgiving, we don't have time to stay here for her to recover tomorrow. She needs a good night's sleep, and so do I.

Though, God knows that won't happen with her by my side.

That means I'm taking the floor tonight.

I carry her through the small room. And lay her gently on the bed. "Get some rest, Princess."

She doesn't respond, just snuggles down and turns slightly onto her side.

I hope she knows if she needs anything, I'll be the one to get it for her. "I'm right here if you need me."

A tiny, contented sigh slips from her open lips, and I reach out and pull the covers up, tucking them around her tightly.

"Goodnight, Princess."

CHAPTER 9

ATHENA

"So, the museum is in the *library*? That's...*interesting*."

By interesting, I mean really odd.

This entire trip along Route 66 has been beautiful but strange. I can see how cool it would have been to travel in its heyday, but now that we're used to all the modern conveniences and luxuries like expressways, some of the sights we're finding along the way have certainly been unexpected.

Like the fact that the Route 66 Museum in Missouri sits in a bright-yellow building that should house books.

Isaiah glances over at me, one eyebrow raised. "You want to go in? If you don't, that's okay. We don't have to."

God, he's so sweet.

After last night, I owe him. Like I didn't already for taking me on this adventure home, but anyone who will hold your hair while you vomit is a solid human being in my book.

For as concerned as Mother and Father—not to mention the *elder* Warrens—are about appearances and ensuring the entire nosy world thinks we're a happy, loving, caring family, one thing they've always struggled with is affection.

I can't even remember the last time anyone besides Artie or Archie gave me a hug because they actually wanted to, rather than for the sake of the cameras or potential on-lookers.

Yet, the man I've known for literally *days* sat on the damn bathroom floor with me, held my hair, and then tucked me in like it was the most natural thing in the world.

The family dynamics over at the Wolfe household are certainly different than at the Warrens.

So, the least I can do is spend a little time at a museum if it's what Isaiah wants.

"Let's go." I sweep out my arm for him to lead the way. "After you."

He chuckles and opens the door, but the ingrained manners prevent him from entering in front of me. His super-manly, old leather smell envelops me, and I can't stop the smile that pulls at my lips as I step inside.

Wow.

I spin around, trying to take in as much as I can of the full-blown 1950s gas station replica just inside. "This is crazy!"

"It is pretty cool, isn't it?" Isaiah wanders around the museum slowly, checking out all the incredible sights—from the gas station to the old cabin and classic diner.

And while he's admiring an old gas pump, I admire him.

My eyes just keep drifting over to him despite my best efforts to remain focused on all the cool items and descriptions surrounding us.

It isn't that they're not interesting—though, I'm sure they're far more so to Isaiah than to me. The jumble of feelings brought on by last night just makes it impossible for me to think about anything else.

He didn't have to do that. My misery was of my own making. The only thing he owes me is to be my holiday fake date since I won the bet. He could have left me to take care of myself, but he didn't. And he didn't complain once or mention the fact that it was my fault I felt so shitty. He acted like he *cared.*

What does that even mean?

My phone ringing prevents me from considering it any further—at least for now. God knows I will be again—and I dig it out of my tiny wristlet.

Shit. Valerie.

"Hey, Isaiah!"

He looks up from the sign he's reading on an exhibit, brow furrowed.

Always so concerned.

I motion toward the phone and jiggle it back and forth. "I need to take this."

If I don't, Valerie is liable to call the cops, or worse…Mother.

"Go ahead." He waves a hand around him. "I'll be here, checking out this stuff."

I hustle out the front door and answer the call before it can go to voicemail. "Hey, girl."

"Don't you 'hey, girl' me! I didn't hear from you yesterday or last night. No proof-of-life text! And I've been calling all damn morning! I was so desperate that I was about to call your family if you didn't answer this time."

"Shit. I'm fine. Really. I'm sorry." I rub my eyes and lean back against the bright-yellow building. "I got sick when we got to the hotel and passed out. And we've been on the road all morning. I didn't mean to make you worry."

"You got sick? Are you okay?"

"Yeah, I'm okay today. I just ate too much and it didn't sit well. How are things there?"

The last thing I want to do is go into any graphic detail about what went down—or came up—last night. Even thinking about it makes my stomach churn.

Valerie sighs at my attempt to change the subject. "First, don't do this again, please. I've thought of every horrible scenario that could possibly happen to you, and it hasn't been pretty. You can't go M.I.A. on a girl who indulges in murder mysteries. Second, in response to your question, things are okay here. My brother and his band are living it up, of course. Every girl on the campus is going crazy for them."

"Kind of what I anticipated."

"So, other than getting sick, how's the trip?"

"Actually, it's good."

Despite the desert squatting, sore ass and legs, and the violent upheaval just hours ago, the past few days have been some of the best I can remember in any recent history.

"We're at a museum right now in Missouri and are heading to St. Louis for the night. It's pretty interesting. How about you? Have you taken a break from studying at all and actually enjoyed your time off?"

"Well, yes, believe it or not." Valerie laughs, likely because she has books and papers spread out around her and has been working herself silly while everyone around her parties. "My brother forced me out to see them play, but I'd rather hear about the hot, homeless guy."

I snicker at the nickname she gave him after I texted her a pic of him that I snuck on day one. "He's actually really nice, and check this out—I made a bet with him and I won! He's going to come to spend Thanksgiving with my family as my fake boyfriend."

A long moment of silence passes before Valerie finally responds. "Athena, you can't be serious. You don't know this guy. Why would you spend more time with him and subject him to your family's antics?"

I push off the wall and peek in the glass door at Isaiah, who has his back to me while he examines something. "I know enough about him after all the time we've spent together on the road, and you know the whole 'keep my parents off my back' thing is kinda high on my priority list to survive this weekend."

She releases a long sigh, her worry coming through the line loud and clear. "Well, just be careful. You don't know this guy."

But I do.

I can't tell Valerie that—she would freak out for sure—but Isaiah has proven to me that he's a good man. He wouldn't do anything to hurt me.

"Okay, girl, I need to go. I promise to send you my proof-of-life texts, and I'll try to call you in a day or two and check-in."

Valerie's laugh trickles through the line. "Yes, please do. Don't make me call your parents, young lady."

Our laughs melt together at the thought of calling the Warrens. She knows how last-resort that would be for me and *should be* for her.

"Don't you dare!"

"I would never do that to you. I wouldn't do that to *anyone*."

"Okay. Talk soon."

I disconnect the call and find my way back into the museum to find Isaiah. Passing by the various exhibits, a sense of nostalgia for a simpler time settles over me. Even though life may have been a bit harder without modern conveniences, things didn't seem so complicated back then.

And the man standing across the room is making this trip very complicated for me.

ISAIAH

Athena doesn't need to announce her return from taking the call. As soon as she gets close, the citrusy scent hits me and my entire body becomes very aware of her presence.

I turn toward her and find her just inside the entrance to the exhibit. "Everything okay?"

She nods and slowly crosses the room toward me. "Yep. Just my roommate checking in."

"To make sure I didn't murder you?"

Her lips curve into an almost seductive smile, and she nods again. "Exactly."

It's such a relief to see her feeling better today after being so damn sick last night. She shouldn't have eaten all that. And she didn't need to. I just didn't have the heart to tell her I would have gone along with her plan regardless—all she had to do was ask. There was no need to add insult to her injury. The woman was determined to prove a point—that she could beat me. I needed to let her have that win for her own ego.

And she needs my support at Thanksgiving dinner. I wouldn't leave her hanging—not ever. After Artie left the family business and Archie married his secretary, it has no doubt left a lot of added pressure to fall on Athena's tiny shoulders.

I know all about pressures. The kind that sent me on this cross-country trip in the first place. The kind that would lead her to want to use me as a decoy at Thanksgiving dinner. Families like the Warrens expect a certain standard to be maintained. And dressed like this, looking like this, I am so far outside of it, it is sure to set them off. They are probably conspiring to set her up with some country club, trust fund boy who meets their approval, and clearly, she wants no part of it. I can't blame her. It's the type of thing that makes you want to rebel, like hopping on a bike and traveling across the country with a stranger.

She looks around at the exhibits and shrugs. "Where are we headed next? Another steak challenge?" She cringes. "Ugh, I was trying to joke about it but even mentioning it is giving me the meat sweats."

"The meat sweats, huh?" I chuckle. "Maybe we grab a salad before we pack it in for the night. We're headed to Saint Louis. I thought we might take a walk, check out the Arch, if you're up for it."

"Yeah, that sounds good. No meat, though…" Her eyes flash with horror. "Promise?"

I chuckle at her again and shake my head. She is really cute today—with her nose scrunched up in disgust and her hand on her jutted hip like she means business.

I cross my fingers in an *X* over my heart. "No meat."

"Okay, Bikes, take us to the Arch."

I offer her a little mock bow. "Your wish is my command, Princess."

She glowers at me, but it's playful. It seems she isn't as annoyed by the nickname as she used to be.

We head toward the museum's exit, and I hold open the door to let her pass through. That citrus smell hits me, and I inhale as casually as I can.

Athena stops dead in her tracks and turns around with her eyebrows up to her hairline. "Bikes, did you just sniff me?"

I fight off a grin. "Nah, it's my allergies."

"Oh, okay." Her eyes narrow slightly. "Sorry. I thought… well, never mind about what I thought."

She turns, shaking her head, and continues moving toward the motorcycle. I do my best not to laugh.

What in the hell possessed me to sniff her?

Apparently, this is what I've been reduced to. A sniffer.

Good lord, I hope Jacob never catches wind of this. He'd never let me live it down.

We start putting on our gear, and even though I know she doesn't need my help, I take the pink helmet from her hands and put it on top of her head.

"Let me make sure this is on."

She smiles up at me from under her thick, dark lashes and bites her bottom lip.

Damn, she's sexy.

Too sexy for her own good. Or mine. Riding with her on my bike is like the longest cocktease in history. But I won't cross that line with her. I need to play her fake boyfriend in New York, not want to be her real one.

I finish tucking the strap through the latch and shoot her my best panty-melting smile. "All good, Princess."

"Thank you. Glad to know that I'm in such good hands."

I'll be damned if she doesn't shoot me a wink before moving to the saddlebag that contains her items.

I stand struck stupid and watch her tuck her tiny purse inside. My eyes drift to the way her jeans hug her perfect hips and butt, then force myself to turn away.

If I don't get my head out of my *ass, I may do something stupid.*

We hop on my bike and head back toward the highway. Athena holds on tight for a bit—which I cannot say I don't enjoy—but she relaxes her grip before long. Holding my waist with one hand, she waves the other in the air and shouts something I can't quite make out.

I glance in my mirror on the handlebar, and her beautiful smile is unmistakable and says everything.

Athena feels the freedom that only the open road and two wheels can offer. Hopping on a motorcycle will cure almost anything, temporarily. It's as if your troubles blow away on the wind.

I hope for Athena's and my own sake that ours do the same and that we aren't riding straight for them.

CHAPTER 10

ATHENA

"Wow! It's so much bigger than I realized." I wiggle my eyebrows and bump my shoulder into Isaiah's arm. "That's what she said."

His barked laugh floats through the air and makes my skin heat.

He has the best laugh. Deep and sexy.

If he were a rockstar, he'd be the type who gets bras and panties thrown at him while on stage. The image pops into my head as we stand in the park under the Arch, and I laugh to myself, imagining what his reaction would be.

"What's so funny?"

No way I'm telling him that.

I ignore his question and look up at the Arch again. It's truly spectacular. "I've never been to Saint Louis. Have you?"

It's far more beautiful and inspiring than I realized it would be. Something about the way the light glints off it almost brings tears to my eyes. This is a case of the pictures truly not being able to do it justice. But it is the perfect location to snap one for Val and send a text.

PROOF OF LIFE: IT'S HUGE! *THAT'S WHAT SHE SAID*

Isaiah peeks at my text and grins. "Yes, I've been here before. My parents loved to take my brothers and me on vacations every summer."

Isaiah sticks his hands into his pockets, and we casually stroll along the trail—not in any hurry to get anywhere.

It's so different than my normal life. When I'm at home, I'm expected to be a Warren and rush from one event to another. At school, things aren't much better. I'm either running from class to class or handling things for Mother and Father on the West Coast when a Warren needs to make an appearance and they aren't able to fly out.

"We came to Saint Louis one summer." He pauses a moment to stare at the river. "I remember we rode the riverboat. It was the highlight of the trip for me. It was all I wanted to do. I thought it was so cool. And of course, one of my younger brothers, James, decided the riverboat was as good a place as any to take off all his clothes and run around like a loon. He got naked at the Arch. It was definitely a memorable trip."

"Wait, what? Your brother got naked at the Arch? I need to hear this story."

Isaiah laughs as he recalls the memory, and his smile outshines the Arch. His eyes sparkle with true humor and fondness, and I'm having a hard time focusing on anything this man is saying.

Just like the Arch, he's a fantastic work of art.

"Don't get too excited, Princess." Isaiah winks at me. "He was a toddler."

We both laugh and pass by another couple strolling down the pathway.

"My parents chased him all over the deck of the boat

while he ran around like a little psycho, shouting and yelling. If you ever meet James, you'll find not much has changed. He's still wild and crazy, and my other brother, Jacob, his twin, is entirely his opposite. They are nothing alike beyond their looks."

If I ever meet James.

That part didn't go unnoticed by me. And the thought of meeting his family makes warmth bloom in my chest. It shouldn't. I shouldn't care. But I do. And this shouldn't feel so much like a *date,* but my hand tingles, waiting for him to reach out and take it all the same.

We continue to walk the trail, and my curiosity over Isaiah's family gets the better of me.

He mentioned working for the family company, and it sounded like his brothers do, too. Without any drama. A strange concept for me after what's happened with the Warrens the last few years.

But he hasn't really given me any details.

"What exactly does your family company do?"

I don't know why, but an intimate mom and pop place filters into my mind. Maybe a hardware store or mechanic's shop. Both of those seem to fit Isaiah's look and laidback demeanor. I can picture a young Isaiah and his brothers following his every step as they run around a small, quaint office at the back of a shop, having the time of their lives while their loving parents watch with genuine affection in their gazes.

The image I've conjured up suits him. He seems very much to have the American Dream life.

Maybe I was way off on the homeless theory.

Isaiah glances over at me for a second, then rubs his hand along his growing stubble and focuses on the water. "Uh, it's a security company."

He doesn't elaborate.

"In Boston? You still have a hint of an accent."

Isaiah smirks and looks at me from under inky brows and hooded eyes. If that isn't sexy, I don't know what is. The tip of his tongue darts out to wet his bottom lip and all my attention shifts to that one slight movement.

He has kissable lips.

"You can take the kid out of Boston."

I shake those thoughts from my mind. "Right. I get it. New York is a part of me even though I've been at Berkeley for almost four years."

"You seem to have lost your accent, though."

"Ahh, well, maybe my days at private schools chased it away, but the temper is still there. You don't want to see me in traffic. It's not pretty."

We stop walking to lean against the railing and take in the Mississippi, and somehow, things feel different between us. I can't put my finger on it, but there's a shift. Maybe we are finally getting to know each other a bit, but there's always been this natural ease between us.

"I don't doubt it for a second, Princess. You're vicious."

"You flatter me, Mr. Wolfe."

His name rolls off my tongue with a more flirtatious tone than I intended, but I don't mind. Not really. His name *is* sexy. And so is he.

I noticed it the moment we met, but the more time I spend with him, the more I find myself picturing his large, muscled body covering mine in a way that is very much not just as friends.

He steps closer, that familiar scent I now associate completely with Isaiah wrapping around me, and I have to crane my neck back to see into his eyes.

Damn, he's a big guy. A big, sexy as sin man.

"I'd like to do a lot more than flatter you, Ms. Warren."

Oh hell. I don't think I'd mind that, not at all.

ISAIAH

Athena just laughs off my comment as we lean against the railing, looking out over the Mississippi, the Arch at our backs—and coincidentally, a riverboat passing in front of us.

"You have two brothers, right?"

Of course, I already know that—as well as their names and the scandals that have surrounded them recently—but I'd rather hear her take on her family, not what gossip columns can supply.

She nods slowly. "I do. Artie and Archie. They're my best friends, well, besides my roommate, Valerie. I guess that's sort of sad. Is that sad?"

I step closer and look down into her beautiful blue eyes that light up when she talks about her brothers. Clearly, she adores them, and I have no doubt that they adore her, too.

The "I adore Athena club" has one more member.

Standing this close to the beauty of the Mississippi River and the water lapping at the shore beside us, all I can see is her. Her citrusy scent invades my lungs with each breath I take, and my fingers itch to touch her.

Christ, I want to kiss her, right here, right now.

From the way her hooded gaze locks onto mine, she is thinking the same thing.

My princess should always get what she wants.

And I want to kiss her. I want to press my lips to hers and finally know what she tastes like.

"Princess…" The wind shifts, and it blows tendrils of hair into her face. I gently move her soft onyx hair, tucking it behind her ear and using the opportunity to cup her face. "You need to stop looking at me like that."

I gently stroke my fingers along her jaw, and there is nowhere I'd rather be right now than here, with her.

"Like what, Bikes?"

That damn nickname.

She can call me whatever the hell she wants, and I'd still happily answer to it just because it's her.

She's the only one that I'd let get away with this shit.

The sound of her sultry, sexy voice only heightens my attraction to this magnificent woman who looks up at me like I'm the only one who can give her what she needs.

"Like kissing me is the only thing you want right now."

I know I sure want to, but I'd never push her, never assume anything.

She presses her cheek firmer into my hand, and I graze my thumb gently back and forth across her soft cheek. Her skin is so smooth and flawless—absolute perfection. Azure eyes lock onto mine, and the way she's looking at me right now, she takes my breath away.

I've never wanted anything more in my life than to kiss this woman. If I have, I suddenly can't recall it.

Athena swallows thickly. "Maybe it is."

Shit. She wants me to kiss her?

Cupping her face between both palms, I tilt it up even higher, losing myself in her gaze. "Be careful what you ask for, Princess. You just might get it."

She rakes her teeth across her bottom lip, and fuck if I can stop myself from taking this moment for myself. We're still practically strangers, and she doesn't know the truth about me or why I'm driving her across the country. But fuck it. I want this.

Hell, I need this.

It's been a long time since a woman has looked at me like this, and maybe it makes me an asshole, but I like it.

I lean in, closing the distance between us until her breath flutters over my lips.

"Isaiah?"

"Athena?"

Her breath comes out in a small gasp as she realizes this is really about to happen.

Hell yeah, it's going to happen.

I could no more stop this kiss than I could control the setting sun, which shines upon her now, giving her an ethereal glow.

She closes her eyes, and somehow, I already know kissing her once couldn't possibly quench this thirst that I now have for her.

A million kisses wouldn't be enough.

I close my eyes, too, committing every second of this to memory because I just know this moment is important.

"Can't catch me, Mommy!" a tiny voice squeals with delight, and a small little body pushes his way between us, forcing us to let go of one another.

We both look down to find a small, shirtless little boy running between us. He can't be more than three, maybe four at the most.

"Andrew! Stop this instant!" A woman—I'm assuming is his mother—chases behind him, picking up his discarded clothes along the way.

Andrew takes off again, squealing as if this is the greatest moment of his short life. His shoes fly into the air in his wake. No doubt his pants are next. "I'm so fast! No one can catch me!"

His mother rushes past us, racing behind him as apologies spill from her lips.

Athena taps my bicep. "What is it about this arch that makes toddlers shed their clothes?"

We both burst into laughter, the spell of the moment broken.

It's for the best.

If she were to find out I'm not who she believes I am, she might feel taken advantage of, and that's the last thing I'd ever want her to feel.

"Come on, Princess. We need to get some rest. We leave early tomorrow morning for Columbus."

"Okay. Let's head back to the hotel." She shifts away from the railing and glances back at me. "I can't believe we finally have separate rooms."

Yeah, me either.

Sharing a room allowed me to make sure she was safe—plus, I definitely enjoy her company—and our rooms are right next door to each other. It's a good thing, though. I could use some time alone. Having her body pressed to mine all day, and now, this near kiss has left me strangely on edge.

I'm not a pervert or unable to control myself, but a man can only take so much torture before he has to walk away.

We make our way back toward the parking lot, and a strange sense of loss settles over me.

It's crazy. We barely know each other. But the more time we spend together, the more I *want* to know her.

And that's dangerous.

CHAPTER 11

ATHENA

We make our way north and east, and the crisp air signals the shift as much as the change in the scenery along the road. The warm breezes of Texas have long since gone.

It's not the only thing that feels different.

Ever since our almost kiss, every brush of our hands against each other, every look we exchange, all seem to have some sort of hidden meaning I can't quite decipher.

Even as we checked into our separate—but connecting—rooms last night, I couldn't sleep, wondering if there would be a knock on that door between us and what I would do about it if it happened.

Truth be told, I still don't know what I would have done *had* he knocked, but with my hands wrapped firmly around Isaiah's waist now, I know what I want to have happened.

And that scares the ever-loving shit out of me.

The signs for Indianapolis signal that we've reached our lunch stop for the day, and the second spot Isaiah has chosen as things he wants to see. He follows signs for the speedway, and the closer we get to stopping, the tenser my body becomes.

This would be so much easier if I had more experience, if I actually understood how to interpret anything men say or do. But spending the few years of my adulthood I have had trying to concentrate on school instead of boys has left me at a severe disadvantage, especially when Isaiah not only has a decade on me but has probably been with dozens of women.

I cringe even thinking that, but it's a reality I have to consider before I go any further with him. *If* I go any further with him. If that's even what he wants.

Fuck, this is confusing.

We pull into Speedway, and he kills the engine and knocks down the kickstand. I slide off the bike and stretch, arching my back to try to work out some of the kinks the ride from St. Louis this morning has already created.

Isaiah removes his shades and watches me as he climbs off the bike. "You okay?"

I nod. "Yeah, just getting out the kinks."

He gives me that little half-grin of his that always makes my heart flip-flop. "You let me know if you need help."

A warmth creeps over my cheeks, and I turn away from him and dig my purse out of the saddlebag as an excuse to cover up my reaction to his comment.

I pull out my phone from my purse and cringe. "Shit."

"What is it?"

Sighing, I scroll through the list of missed calls and texts, my annoyance increasing with every one. "I need to make a phone call or two and send some texts."

Isaiah inclines his head toward the building. "I'm going to head in, use the bathroom, and check to see if there's anything going on at the track today that we can catch."

"Okay, I'll meet you inside in a couple minutes."

Concerned green eyes watch me for a second and scan the parking lot.

"Go. I'll be fine."

He pulls off his helmet, sets it on the bike, and runs a hand back through his wavy, dark hair. "Okay, Princess, you know where to find me."

I force myself not to watch Isaiah saunter away and instead dial Artie.

Like usual, he answers almost immediately. "Athena?"

"What's the big emergency? You must've called and texted a dozen times, and I have a bunch from Archie and Mother, too."

"Well, hello to you, too."

"Sorry, hi."

"Mother's having an absolute meltdown that you haven't called her once since you left Berkeley. Archie and I have assured her you have texted us and you're fine, but you may just want to give her a call."

I squeeze my eyes closed and pinch the bridge of my nose. "No. Fuck that. Do you know what she's trying to do?"

He releases a heavy sigh. "Let me guess, set you up with one of her friend's kids?"

"Cliff Clifton this time. I'm taking the slow way home to ensure I have as little time there as possible and I have thwarted her plans by bringing my boyfriend with me."

"Your boyfriend?"

I chuckle and lean against the bike. "Well, that's who she's going to *think* he is."

Artie lets out a laugh. "You're playing with fire, sis."

"I know. But Mother has lit a few of her own over the years, so it's time for a little payback. Tell her I'm fine, and I'll probably see her Wednesday night."

"Okay."

"You're going to be there with Penelope and the kids, right?"

"Yes. We'll be there, and so will Archie and Blair. You should call him and maybe warn him about your plans. This should be a fun Thanksgiving."

"That's one way of putting it."

"See you in a few days."

"Love you, bye." I immediately dial Archie and wait while it rings.

"Hey, little sis, I was wondering when you were going to return my calls and texts."

I sigh and roll my eyes even though he can't see me. "I'm on a damn motorcycle, Arch. It's not like I can check my calls and get back to you easily. I just talked to Artie."

"Good. And he told you to call Mom?"

"Of course, he did, but I'm not going to. I told him to let her know I'm fine and that I'll be home for Thanksgiving. That's all she needs to know."

He snorts. "And what are you not telling her?"

I laugh and drop my head back to stare up at the fall blue sky. "That I'm not coming home alone."

"When you say it like that, I can assume it won't be someone she's happy to see?"

"Definitely not. About as happy as she was when you married Blaire."

He chuckles and the phone jostles. "Just remember that the more you antagonize her, the harder she comes down on you."

"Oh, believe me, I've seen it enough over the last two years with you and Artie. It's why I've always made it crystal clear to her that I don't want her meddling in my personal life."

"While I certainly admire your commitment to making sure Mother knows her place, I also need to warn you that being on the receiving end of a full Warren attack isn't a comfortable place to be."

I sigh and rub my eyes. "I know things were hard for you after Artie quit, but you have Blaire now. You have someone who can back you up, no matter what."

"You have that, too, Athena. Artie and I will always do what we can to defend your right to make your own life choices, even if we don't always agree with them. But please, don't do anything *stupid* in the name of rebellion."

"I wouldn't do that."

Would I? Is what I'm contemplating doing with Isaiah stupid?

"You're a smart girl, Athena. Smarter than any of us, if I'm being honest. Just use that big head of yours to make the good decisions so we don't end up having to bail you out of a shitty situation later."

"Fair enough. I'll see you soon. Tell Mother I'm fine."

I end the call and shove my phone into my purse but take a second before I head in after Isaiah.

With everyone around the table this year, including my date, there will definitely be some fireworks.

I just hope I don't get burned by them.

ISAIAH

I reach the Speedway building and turn back one last time to check on Athena before I duck inside and pull out my phone. I'd rather not have to make this call, but they need to know I won't be home for Thanksgiving.

It would be rude not to give some sort of notice, but it also means potentially having to answer questions I don't particularly want to right now. I'm not sure how to explain what's happened with Athena—mostly because I don't understand it myself.

A lie started this, but the longer it goes on, the more real it actually feels with her.

What will that mean when we get to New York and she discovers I'm not Prez272?

I hope she understands why I did it and forgives me for the deception, but it could certainly go another way. Another way I can't even stomach thinking about at the moment.

Instead, I pull up Jacob's number and hit send.

He answers on the second ring. "Hey, bro, you back yet?"

I run a hand over my growing beard, the roughness starting to actually feel normal now when it was so foreign at the start of my trip. "Not yet. I'm in Indianapolis."

"Oh, sweet! Going to stop at the Speedway and take one of the cars out for a spin?"

I chuckle and glance around the lobby of the museum. "I don't think today is one of the racing experience days, nor do I have a reservation. I also don't want to spend too much time here and end up having to ride late tonight."

"Bummer."

"Yeah, well, I'm calling to let you know…"

It's better to just rip off the Band-Aid than to dance around the truth that may hurt. That's especially true where Jacob and James are concerned. They have a way of tag-teaming me and dragging it out of me eventually anyway.

"I'm just calling to let you fuckers know that I'm not going to be home for Thanksgiving."

"What? Why the hell not?"

I sigh and lean against the wall near the glass doors so I can watch Athena and know when she's heading this way. "I have to make a stop in New York for something, and it's going to keep me there through the weekend."

"Dad isn't going to be very happy about you missing Thanksgiving."

While holidays were always important to him and Mom, once she died, they seemed to become even more so. He clings to that special time with us and those family traditions to help keep her memory alive, so missing this will be tough on him *and* me. But Athena needs me, and a bet is a bet.

"I know. But he'll have me back Monday, and you and James can get back to busting my balls like usual then."

"What about me?"

Great. James is there.

Jacob puts me on speakerphone, a light static now coming through in the background. "It's Isaiah. He's not coming home for Thanksgiving. Says he has something to take care of in New York."

James scoffs. "What the hell do you have to do in New York?"

"None of your damn business."

"Oh…that means it isn't business and it *is* personal."

Jacob chuckles. "Since when does Isaiah have a personal life?"

James snorts. "My point exactly. What the hell are you up to, Isaiah?"

I wish I fucking knew.

This whole thing with Athena has gotten a lot more complicated. So have my feelings for her. What started out as a desire to protect her from that scumbag who would take advantage of her on this trip has morphed into a desire for *her.*

"None of your fucking business. I'll be home Monday."

Jacob sighs. "He's going to call you, you know."

"I know." And I'm going to ignore *his* calls as long as possible before I have to deal with that. "By the way, Jacob, guess where I just stopped."

117

He chuckles. "Well, since you're in Indianapolis, my guess is St. Louis last night and the location of James' epic stunt."

"Yep." I laugh and shake my head. "I was standing there, staring at it, and literally, all I could think about was your naked ass."

And kissing Athena, but they don't need to know that part.

James barks out a laugh. "You stop thinking about my ass!"

"Request denied. I'll talk to you assholes later."

I end the call and slip my phone into my pocket just in time to watch Athena make her way across the parking lot toward me, a frown tilting her lips.

She steps through the door, and her gaze lands on me, hard when it's normally so liquid and inviting.

"What's wrong?"

Athena shakes her head and forces a smile that doesn't quite reach her eyes. "Nothing's wrong. Just a reminder of why I'm doing this trip."

"Your mother?"

Her perfect bow lips twist into a scowl as she brushes past me. "Who else? Let's go see some cars."

She rushes off like a fire's been lit under her ass, apparently eager to put some space between herself and whatever conversation she just had, but she stops next to an Indy car in the main lobby and snaps a selfie with it.

"Another proof-of-life shot for your friend?"

"Yep." She taps at her screen and hits send before slipping it back into her pocket. "I don't need the cops coming, or even worse, the Warrens, to come looking for me."

"What did this one say?"

"Reached Indianapolis. Going to see if they'll lend me this car for the drive home after Thanksgiving dinner is over."

I bark out a laugh and shake my head, ushering her

farther into the building. "Because you can't get away from your family fast enough?"

"Something like that."

Whatever is going on between Athena and her parents definitely has her on edge. I would do anything to help her relieve the stress and maybe dissipate some of the tension, but something tells me I might just be another source of it for her.

Hopefully, a little time here before we hop on the bike and make our way to Columbus does her—and me—some good.

CHAPTER 12

ISAIAH

"They're so *cute!*" Athena snaps a photo and quickly sends off a text, undoubtedly to her friend, as proof we've made it safely to our next stop in Columbus.

I follow Athena's gaze to make sure I'm looking at the same thing she is. Tilting my head doesn't do anything to change what I'm seeing. "I'm not sure that's the word I would use to describe them. Maybe *massive* or *majestic?*"

Athena scrunches up her brow and considers my suggestions while she examines the elephants in the paddock at the Columbus Zoo. "I guess *majestic* works, too." She offers an almost forlorn sigh and leans against the railing. "I just love the way the mother closely watches and cares for her baby."

Her eyes mist over slightly, and she shifts her stance as if uncomfortable with her own observation and shivers in the chilling fall air. Given everything she's told me during our trip, it's pretty clear she's thinking about her relationship with her own mother.

I nudge her with my shoulder. "You know, not all mothers have the same kind of relationship with their children. Some are close. Some aren't. Doesn't mean there isn't love there."

I've experienced it myself with Dad, but I've never once doubted that everything he does is out of his love for me and the twins. Mom was the one who comforted us and played the caregiver role because he was always busting his ass at the office to ensure the company was productive, but we never questioned that he loved us. He just showed us in different ways that sometimes took us a while to recognize.

Athena scowls and crosses her arms over her chest. "Some try to control you and dictate your life."

I chuckle, knowing that common scenario all too well, even if Mom and Dad really tried not to with us. "Some do. But I have a hard time believing you let anyone tell you what to do."

She peeks at me out of the corner of her eye, humor twinkling in the blue, and smirks. "Wherever did you get that idea?"

The playfulness has returned to her mood, and I lean down and brush my lips against her ear, letting her crisp, citrusy scent invade every inhale I take.

"Maybe it was watching you inhale a seventy-two-ounce steak just because I didn't think you could do it."

She turns her head toward me, almost brushing her lips against mine. A steely resolve settles in her blue eyes. "Yeah, and I beat your ass."

"And paid for it later."

Something I wish hadn't needed to happen, but at least she seems like she's able to joke about it, which is good.

Athena turns away and goes back to watching elephants, and her reminding me of our little bet pushes our impending meeting with the Warren clan to the forefront of my mind.

I need to get the lay of the land and know what I'm walking into, beyond what she's already told me about the tensions in the household. "There anything I should know before we arrive in New York? Anything about your family? Things I shouldn't mention?"

Not that I plan on striking up any in-depth conversations with the Warrens if I can avoid it, but there are certain subjects that are touchy in every family that people from outside wouldn't think they need to dance around. If I at least have some warning, I can try to stay away from those topics and stick to more pleasant ones.

She snort-laughs and shakes her head. "You're liable to set off my mother or father *or* my grandfather with just about any topic." She glances at me. "But my grandmother can be cool, and my brothers will probably love you once they move past your appearance."

I let my jaw drop in mock indignation. "What's wrong with my appearance?"

"Shit." She bites her bottom lip and shifts nervously, averting her gaze. "Well, nothing really. It's just…" She finally looks back at me, her eyes traveling from my dirty motorcycle boots up over my jeans and jacket to my beard and tousled hair. "You look like a dirty, potentially homeless transient."

Potentially homeless?

Transient?

I bark out a laugh and cross my arms over my chest defensively. "So, it's not just about your wanting them to know you rode all the way there on a motorcycle. You want me to go because you think my appearance is going to freak them out."

Clever.

There was a time when I might have done the same thing and brought home a woman who appeared to operate in the world's oldest profession to get a rise out of the old man, but I've outgrown my youthful desire to push boundaries to the breaking point.

And she's probably right about how I look right now. I rub a hand across what is no longer scruff and has become more like a beard. Riding across the country on a motorcycle isn't easy on the body, and I've done it twice now in the span of a month.

She grabs my bicep and squeezes gently. "I didn't mean to—"

I step into her until our chests almost touch. A flush creeps up her neck and over her cheeks, just as it has before. I lean forward and brush my lips against her ear, wrapping my hand around her shoulder to pull her against me fully. "It's okay to admit that you like me, Princess. I like you, too."

Actually saying the words we've both been feeling is like a weight being lifted off my shoulders and another one settling right in its place. Because now there'll be no more dancing around the subject, no more pretending that we're not attracted to each other in a way that's very different from how this all started.

"Do you like me, Athena? As more than your cross-country chauffeur?"

One of the elephants trumpets. And Athena jerks away from me and clears her throat as another couple who looks happy and disgustingly in love passes. "I think you already know the answer to that question."

ATHENA

Another couple slowly passes us along the path through the zoo, hand in hand, smiling at each other like two fools in love. It gives me a second to regain my breath and find my bearings after Isaiah just about knocked me off my feet by flat-out asking me that.

And looking into his warm green eyes, I don't want to lie, but I also can't bring myself to say the words. "I think you already know the answer to that question."

Isaiah smirks at me and shrugs nonchalantly. "I might or I might not. Just because I feel that way certainly doesn't mean you do, too."

Holy shit. Did he just admit that everything I've been feeling isn't one-sided? That all the playful banter and lingering touches are completely intentional on his part?

As if the heat of my earlier blush wasn't enough, it rushes through me again with a vengeance—a burning-hot wave of lust and embarrassment. And standing here like this, in the cool evening air under the soft overhead lights, sets the mood for something far more than friendship.

Something I don't know if I'm ready for even though everything about Isaiah draws me to him instead of pushing me away.

I clear my throat and take a step back from the man driving me absolutely crazy on so many levels. "Come on, I want to go see the penguins."

He chuckles softly at my abrupt change in subject and follows me slowly down the path. Settling in next to me, his large, warm palm finds mine, and he squeezes it gently.

Oh, God. I hope he can't tell how much my body is shaking.

I can't even remember the last time a boy held my hand. Probably back when it actually was a boy. But Isaiah is far from that. He's a real man. Ten years my senior and has probably done things in bed I can't even imagine.

Why would he be interested in someone like me?

Money is the obvious answer. He may not have known

who I was when I posted as GoddessA, looking for a ride, but he likely did the moment he saw me. Or, at the very least, soon after.

If I were being cynical, it would be easy to believe his only motive is financial, but he's given me no reason to question him or his intentions. This man casually strolling with me, hand clasped firmly in his, has been nothing but a complete and utter gentleman the entire time, so I push those concerns to the back of my mind and enjoy the feeling of his warm palm against mine, holding it possessively.

I never thought I would be one of those girls who got joy out of being with a man, likely from a lack of good role models. I don't doubt that Grandmother and Grandfather and Mother and Father care for each other, but the complete lack of affection always struck me as so cold. If that's what a healthy relationship looks like, I never want it.

But the last few years, seeing Artie find Penelope and Max and Archie and Blaire find each other and settle down has proven to me that I'm doing the right thing in thwarting Mother's plans for me. If I had caved and done what she wanted, I never would've met Isaiah and I wouldn't be here tonight like this with him.

Though, I'm not exactly sure what any of this means.

What will happen when the holidays are over and we return to Berkeley?

We haven't talked about school much, mostly because it's the last thing I *want* to think about while I'm on this little break.

I peek over at him. "So, what are your plans after Thanksgiving? Are you going to head back to Berkeley right away?"

He stiffens slightly next to me and rubs his jaw with his free hand, glancing at some of the other animals as we stroll along. "I'm not completely sure of my plans yet. I may have to stay in Boston for a while. Family stuff."

My heart sinks to the pit of my stomach. "Oh, so you're dropping out of school?"

He chews on the side of his cheek for a moment. "I already have a bachelor's, and I don't really need anything else to work for the family business."

"Oh…I see…"

His answer makes bile rise up my throat.

When would I see him again?

I swallow the question down thickly as we approach the penguins. He releases my hand and leans against the fence, resting his forearms on it.

A heavy silence spans between us for a moment while the arctic birds slide on the rocks, then he glances over at me. "You like penguins?"

I nod and watch them swimming through the water in the exhibit, zipping back and forth playfully. It reminds me of swimming with Artie and Archie in Cape Harmony when I was little, but Mother and Father never brought us back after that summer Artie spent with Penelope. "I'm not sure why. They've just always looked so peaceful and gentle."

Isaiah nods. "They sure do."

"Like they live a good life here. Without fear of being attacked by sea lions or polar bears out on the ice caps. They're taken care of here. They know they'll get fed and have a beautiful place to live."

It's more than I can say.

If my little stunt with bringing Isaiah home for Thanksgiving doesn't make them come down on me harder than they did with Artie and Archie and cut me off, then my telling them about my plans after graduation certainly will. In only a few months, my world is going to look a lot different.

I sigh and mimic Isaiah's positioning against the railing. "Too bad our lives aren't so black and white."

He slowly turns his head to look at me and offers me a sad smile. "Couldn't have said it better myself, Princess."

CHAPTER 13

ISAIAH

Even though I'm going to spend the next couple of days in Manhattan with the Warrens, today almost feels like the end.

In some ways, it is. Our last day riding together. Our last day on the open road. The last chance I'll get to spend any time with Athena when she is happy and carefree. Because I know as soon as we pull into her parents' driveway, all hell is going to break loose.

Seeing her so upset last night at the zoo made me realize just how tense things really are between her and her mother, in particular. And I can't help but feel for her. To be twenty-one, just setting out in life, preparing to graduate and start your future, but having no say in it—or at least feeling like you don't—must be excruciating for her.

It was always expected that I would come work for the family. If I had chosen not to, Dad would have been disappointed. But no one would've pushed me. No one would have threatened me or tried to force me into it by any means necessary. And Mom and Dad certainly never would have tried to interfere with my personal life. Given what went down very publicly with her two brothers over the last few years and was splashed all over the tabloids, I have a feeling the Warrens are the exact opposite.

They're the types who feel that interfering in their kids' lives is a God-given right and one they won't ever back down from. I've seen it happen with my friends before, and it never sat well with me. But seeing what it's doing to Athena almost makes me want to drive this bike right to Boston, where she can spend the holiday with a family that won't do that. Too bad that isn't an option.

Athena's rebellious streak may spell trouble for her future, and that makes me want to use this one last day to really make sure she has fun and do something I'm certain she'll enjoy before we hit New York tonight.

She deserves it, and I want to be the one to give it to her.

The open road always does a lot to soothe any aches in my soul, but the closer we get to our final destination, the more tense she becomes. Thankfully, I think our midday stop is going to turn her attitude around—at least for a little while. I don't think anyone could set foot inside there and *not* immediately flip into a good mood.

As we start seeing the signs for the place I picked, she shifts behind me and leans forward to yell over the engine and road noise. "Hershey?"

I can barely hear her, but I know what she's asking and nod in response. She practically bounces off the seat behind me with excitement and presses her lips to the back of my exposed neck. It sends a shiver down my spine and makes me adjust my position on the seat for a whole other reason.

All the tension that's been building between us hasn't boiled over yet. Things keep getting in the way—whether they be little naked boys or harsh feelings about her mother, the time has just never been right.

So, to feel her lips on me—even just there—makes my heart thrash violently in my chest.

It should be a warning. A drum indicating the coming war with the Warrens that's bound to happen. But I ignore it as we pull up outside the Hershey factory and Athena's small hands tighten around my waist with her excitement.

She practically leaps off the bike the second I throw down the kickstand, her jaw hanging open. "Oh, my God."

I shut down the engine, and she bounces up and down on her feet, clapping her hands and looking every bit as young as she is.

Her wide eyes meet mine, and she grins. "This is the best idea, Isaiah. I absolutely love chocolate."

I smirk at her and slide off the bike, pulling off my helmet. "I don't know any woman who doesn't."

Athena gives me a little playful scowl as she removes her helmet and places it on the seat. "I don't need to hear about all the other women you've been here with, Isaiah."

She moves to turn toward the saddlebag to grab her purse, but I reach out to capture her wrist and drag her up against me.

"I've never been here before, Princess, let alone with another woman." I lean down until my lips almost brush against hers. "Despite what you may think, there haven't been that many women. There hasn't been one in a very long time."

No time for one and no interest in wasting what little time I did have with someone who was in it for the wrong reasons.

A tiny little breath puffs from her lips, and she locks her blue gaze with mine, a blush spreading over her pale cheeks

—so stark against her black hair hanging around her face. "Oh."

I raise an eyebrow. "*Oh?* That's the only thing you have to say?"

For some reason, I thought revealing that to her would make her feel better about our flirting, help her realize what's happening between us isn't just some everyday thing. But this stubborn girl seems intent on leaving me hanging.

I guess I can do the same for her...

She nods slowly, and I duck my head closer, as if I'm going to kiss her, then freeze just before our lips meet.

"Okay, Princess." I back away from her, and she almost falls forward, leaning toward me. I chuckle and grab her hand. "Let's go."

She snags her purse, snaps a picture with the building behind and fires off a text, likely to Val, and lets me drag her across the parking lot toward the factory.

Not that I didn't want to kiss her back there. I wanted it more than *anything*. But from what I've seen, she's a girl who's used to getting what she wants easily, and it's so much more fun to make this a game and toy with her.

She has to learn that good things come to those who wait. Something tells me this is going to be a very good day and a very frustrating one at the same time.

ATHENA

Who knew chocolate could be so sexy?

Though everyone knows it's supposed to be an aphrodisiac, I've never experienced it personally. Until today.

The tour ride that was absolutely meant to be wholesome family fun somehow turned into an opportunity for

Isaiah to wrap one strong arm around me and use the other to brush lightly along my thigh in a way that made me squirm the entire time. And now, walking around the gift shop, his hand wrapped tightly around mine, my entire body buzzes with anticipation for something that hasn't come yet.

We've been so damn close to kissing that I can practically feel his lips on mine every time he looks at me. But it hasn't happened, and the wait is killing me almost as much as my ass was that first day of riding.

Isaiah squeezes my hand. "You okay?"

"Huh?" I turn away from the display in the gift shop and meet his concerned gaze.

"You seemed a million miles away just now."

"Oh…"

Busted.

I motion toward the shelf in front of me. "I was just wondering what possessed them to create a key lime pie flavored Kit-Kat."

He barks out a laugh and grabs one with his free hand. "I mean, I like key lime pie."

"So do I, but I don't know that it belongs in a chocolate bar."

That lazy smirk spreads across his lips. "Fair enough, but you should give it a chance. You might end up liking it."

Is he talking about the candy bar or him?

It could be either, and the way his green eyes assess me now, I'm thinking it's the latter. I never did answer his question about whether I liked him or not. Saying it out loud makes all this real when right now, it feels like some dream. Even with everything that has gone wrong, the rest feels *right.* But I don't have to say the words for him to know.

He drops his head toward me, brushing his rough, bearded cheek against mine and settling his warm lips to my ear. His grip on my hand tightens, and his hot breath flutters against my skin. "We could try it together later, Princess."

Shit.

A full-body shudder rolls through me, and I tug my hand out of his so he won't feel the sweat that's breaking out on my palms.

His dark eyebrows rise slowly. "Is that a no?"

"Can I help you two find anything?" A far-too-perky salesperson steps up next to us with a plastered-on smile.

I turn toward her, once again ignoring Isaiah's question because I have no dang idea how to answer it. "I think we're good. Thank you."

Isaiah offers me a little grin as she walks away, and he grabs a bunch of different candy bar flavors from the shelf. "We'll take this up later, Princess." He leans in again. "When we don't have an audience or any interruptions."

Holy hell.

Over the past few hours, I've been able to forget where we'll be tonight—under the Warren estate roof. Isaiah has done his best to take my mind off the impending drama showing up with him is sure to create, but now, visions of sneaking into his room or him sneaking into mine once the lights go out flood my mind.

I've never wanted anything so much or feared it so much in my entire life.

Things are so unsettled, so up in the air. He doesn't even know if he's coming back to Berkeley after Thanksgiving. I don't know when or even *if* I'll ever see him again after he drives away from me on Sunday, but none of that seems to matter to my heart or body that both yearn to be in his arms. To experience *all* of the man I've spent the most of the last week with my arms wrapped around, traveling across the country.

I watch him cross the gift shop and grab a few other small

items. We definitely don't have much room in the saddlebags for anything else, but it seems he's a man on a mission.

He strolls back over toward me casually and smiles. "Spread your beautiful lips."

"Excuse me?"

Heat coils low in my belly and spreads through my limbs as Isaiah looks at me like he's about to devour me.

"Your mouth." He steps closer and raises his hand, a small piece of chocolate poised between two fingers. "Open it."

I do as he orders, slowly opening my mouth while keeping my gaze locked with his. His fingertips brush my lips, sending a little buzz through me before the chocolate slips between them and hits my tongue.

Bitter, sweet, salty, and with the richness of almonds, it dances across my palate, and a moan slips out before I can swallow it with the candy.

Isaiah's eyes darken, and he leans in again. "If you're going to keep making sounds like that, Princess, I'll feed you chocolate all night long."

Damn.

I'd let him.

Despite all the reasons it's probably a bad idea, I can't deny that it's what I want. That *he* is what I want. My fake Thanksgiving date has somehow become the man I want to be my *real* one.

I swallow the sweet treat, along with all the fantasies raging in my head. "That was amazing."

Isaiah offers me a wink. "I bet it was." His mouth hit mine before I can brace myself for impact. Slow and sweet at first, the kiss almost instantly shifts to something else, his tongue slipping out to play along the seam of my lips. And just as quickly as he kissed me, he pulls away with a smirk. "I just wanted to know what that tastes like on your lips, Princess."

He saunters away to the checkout to pay for whatever

other torture items he has in his hands while leaving me on unsteady legs. Or maybe it's the ground that's unsteady.

It seems that since that night I walked into Whiskey Jack's and first met Isaiah, everything in my life has been off-kilter. While things never seem to change when it comes to the Warrens and my relationship with Mother and Father, things with Isaiah have warped from road-trip partner to friend to God only knows what in just a matter of days.

I could try to blame it on the close proximity, having to wrap my body around his all day on that bike, but that would be ignoring the very real truth that I just feel connected to Isaiah—on far more than a physical level.

He doesn't expect anything from me. Doesn't demand I act a certain way or follow certain rules. He lets me make my own mistakes—like eating a meal big enough to feed a small country just to prove a point. He challenges me and lets me just *be*.

That's something I can't remember ever having with *anyone*, let alone a guy who was actually interested in me. It's what Artemis and Archimedes found in Penelope and Blaire. That *thing* everyone seeks.

And I'm feeling all this before he does anything more than kiss me.

When he finally does something more, when things finally cross that invisible line I've held onto so tightly my entire life, I'm not sure where it will go or where it will leave me.

Hopefully, somewhere as good as that chocolate he just fed me.

CHAPTER 14

ATHENA

They say that New York is the city that never sleeps. Well, even if Mother and Father *were* sleeping, there's no way they are now. Whether intentional or not, Isaiah revs the engine on his bike and races us up the circular driveway fast enough to have me clinging to him for dear life.

Though, I don't need the extra reason to cling to him more tightly.

The rest of the time we spent in Hershey only drew us together more. The flirty comments. The looks he gave me like he wanted to swallow me whole. Right now, I would definitely let him. But first, I have to deal with what is likely to be a very annoyed Bunny Warren and Artemis Warren, the second.

Isaiah pulls us to a stop in front of the steps leading up to the double front doors, and they fly open before we can even climb off the bike.

Father's shrewd, icy-blue gaze cuts through me the same

way it always has, and Mother scowls and crosses her arms, pulling her robe more tightly around her.

She glances at Isaiah, and even though it looks like a casual perusal, I have no doubt she's taking in every speck of dirt on him, every worn portion of his leather jacket, every minute detail. "Athena Warren! What the hell do you think you're doing? It's almost midnight." Her eyes flicker to the motorcycle. "Is this how you got home? On the back of some ruffian's bike?"

Isaiah squeezes my hands gently where they rest against his stomach, offering me silent but important support. I slide off the bike and pull off the helmet before I set it onto the seat and force a saccharine-sweet smile at the woman who gave birth to me.

"It's nice to see you, too, Mother. Father..." I incline my head toward him, but he barely acknowledges the gesture, instead keeping his gaze locked on Isaiah as he climbs from the bike and pulls off his helmet to hang it from the handlebars.

Mother glowers at me, her annoyance level rising the longer I continue to ignore her question.

Good.

Let her wait. Let her anger fester for as long as possible before the inevitable showdown. It gives me a few extra moments to steel myself for it.

She glances from Isaiah to me. "Athena, you rode home with this..." She turns up her nose as if she's smelled something foul. "Man?"

I grab my things from the saddlebag and ignore her again until I have everything and can slowly make my way up the stairs to her. "I did, Mother, and he has a name. It's Isaiah. And he's my boyfriend. He'll be joining us for Thanksgiving dinner and spending the weekend here."

Her eyes widen, her jaw dropping incredulously. "You can't be serious."

"Oh, but I am, Mother." I lean in and press a kiss to her cheek. "Happy Thanksgiving."

Her lips open and close several times, but no sound comes out except an exasperated whine.

I stop next to Father and push up to my tiptoes to press a kiss to his cheek. "Goodnight, Father."

"Athena." The cool reply matches the ice in his gaze.

He's never been an overly affectionate man, but tonight is a whole different level—even for him.

It shouldn't come as a surprise, but my gut still tightens as I make my way inside. Isaiah grabs his bag from the bike and follows quickly up the steps.

"Athena, my darling."

I jerk my head toward the sound of Grandmother's voice as she descends the staircase.

"I was worried you weren't going to make it tonight."

Her tight embrace wraps me in warmth and comfort I hadn't known I needed, and her chest rumbles slightly with her chuckle. "I see you brought a friend. An attempt to avoid your mother's set-up?"

I pull back and catch the slight twitch of a smile on her lips. She winks at me and steps forward, extending her hand toward Isaiah, who has followed me inside with Mother hot on his heels.

Grandfather watches from halfway down the stairs, his shrewd gaze traveling over Isaiah and me, but he doesn't say anything. I offer him a little wave and half-smile, then a harsh hand grasps my elbow and whips me backward.

"Athena?" Mother tightens her grip. "Did you really think you could just walk in with a complete stranger after ignoring my calls for a week and there wouldn't be any consequences?"

I scowl at her but don't bother dignifying her question with an answer. I've pushed their boundaries and expectations my entire life—unlike Artie and Archie, who only really did it recently. She should have expected I wouldn't follow along with her plan for my time home at Thanksgiving so easily.

"I have Cliff Clifton coming over for drinks tomorrow after he finishes his family dinner."

"I suggest you cancel those plans, Mother. It might make it a little bit awkward for Isaiah and me."

Her jaw drops, and she shakes her head. "I don't know where you get this attitude from. It's unacceptable."

It's the same argument I've had with her since I was old enough to remember. The woman expects to get her way—or "there will be consequences"—and I've never been the pushover she expects me to be because I'm female and a Warren.

"I had planned on spending the night here, Mother, so I could sleep in my own bed and have more time with the family, but I can see that Isaiah and I aren't welcome." I turn back toward him, and a flicker of movement at the top of the staircase diverts my attention.

Artie stands at the top with baby Persephone wrapped in his arms, Archie beside him, both watching what unfolds below. I throw a little wave at them before I grab Isaiah's arm.

"Talk to you guys tomorrow."

They both offer me a nod of support, and I drag Isaiah into the house, toward the back door.

Mother rushes after me, her normally stoic face twisted in panic. "Where do you think you're going?"

"The boathouse." I stop at the back door and face her. "If you want to continue to dig into me, you can do it tomorrow. I've had a long day on the road and need sleep." I open the back door and motion for a stunned-looking Isaiah to exit in front of me. Holding the handle, I turn back toward Mother. "You know, after what happened with Artie and Archie, I would've thought you had learned that you can't always get what you want and that pushing us, trying to cram us into the mold you have in place for us is only sure to push us away further. But"—I shrug—"apparently not."

With those words heavy in the air between us, I pull the door closed behind me and motion for Isaiah to follow me across the massive patio and out onto the manicured lawn.

"Where are we going?" It's the first thing he's said since we've arrived.

But I appreciate that he didn't try to step in and be my Superman when it came to the family. That would have only increased the tension.

I point toward the boathouse across the lawn, near the water. "That's where we're going."

"You okay, Princess?" Concern deepens his voice.

I heave out a harsh sigh and glance at him. "No. But I will be."

ISAIAH

Even by the moonlight overhead and the occasional garden lights scattered across the lawn, the frustration and annoyance on Athena's face are impossible to miss.

I can't blame her.

That confrontation with her mother was uncomfortable for me, so I can only imagine what it was like for her. Athena knew exactly what she was doing when she jumped on the back of my bike. Even though she intended this entire battle with her mother, I don't think she anticipated how difficult it truly might be, how much it might hurt her to see the disappointment in Bunny Warren's gaze.

She storms toward the building at the water's edge, her shoulders tense, her lips twisted into a frown.

"Slow down, Princess. We aren't in any rush."

She glances over her shoulder at me and huffs. "I want to put as much distance between that woman and me as I can, while I can. Because as soon as the sun comes up, I'm not going to be able to avoid her anymore."

I chuckle and shake my head.

Fair enough.

Athena reaches the door and enters a code on the keypad to unlock it. Her blue eyes finally spark with humor as she grips the handle and pushes open the door. "Our accommodations for the night."

I pause before I enter, searching her face for any regret over her decision to walk away. "You sure you don't want to go back and talk? I think there are some things that need to get resolved."

"No." She shakes her head, sending her dark hair shifting around her face. "I need a little space." A long, heavy sigh slips from Athena's lips. "I forget how vicious she can be. I'm sorry about what she said back there."

I push a strand of dark hair back from her face to cup her cheek. "You don't need to apologize for your mother. Even though I know it's not how you see it right now, I'm going to suggest something that will sound crazy—that she was just trying to protect you because she cares and she loves you."

She snorts and leans into my touch slightly. "She was trying to protect the *family*. She's going to have to call the Cliftons and cancel the little set-up, and that's a huge embarrassment for her. Plus, I'm sure seeing me roll up on your bike and knowing I chose that over our private jet was a massive blow to her ego."

I brush my thumb across her soft cheek. "Probably."

"Please, I don't want to talk about my mother anymore." She raises a dark eyebrow at me. "Do you?"

"No, I'd rather not."

She offers me a little grin. "Good."

Yes. Very good.

"After you, Bikes."

She motions for me to enter in front of her, and I smirk and drop my hand from her cheek.

"Whatever you say, Princess."

I step into the dark building, and Athena clicks on the switch, illuminating two boats floating in the lapping water. Even down here, where things are utilitarian, it's still nicer than some of the places we've stayed on this trip.

She motions to the side. "This way."

I let her lead me up the stairs. Not because I couldn't have figured out where to go on my own, but because watching her tight ass in the jeans that are practically painted on is too tempting an opportunity to pass up. Even though we just had a very uncomfortable confrontation, my hands itch to reach out and grab her every step she takes.

Down boy. This isn't the time.

She pauses at the top of the stairs and glances back at me before I follow her into a loft that rivals the Drakeston Hotel.

Heavy, expensive leather furniture fills the space along with nautical-themed items that appear to have been carefully selected—either by Bunny or a hired designer. But my eyes drift to a shelf filled with trophies on one wall.

I set down my bag and make my way over there. "What are these?"

She lowers her bag to the wooden floors and peeks over her shoulder at me. "Oh, my brothers' trophies. They both used to row crew in high school and college. They were

143

pretty good, too. Kills Father and Grandfather that neither of them does it anymore."

I chuckle and shake my head as I run my finger along the shelf that somehow has zero dust. Not that I would expect anything less from the Warren matriarch. Even though Athena's grandmother is still alive, something tells me Bunny does her best to take that role and hold onto it for dear life.

Athena lets out a sigh and drops onto the couch, probably shooting off a text to Val to tell her we arrived, then leans down and undoes her boots, kicking them across the room unceremoniously. She sags back across the leather and offers me a little half-smile. "I know you said not to apologize, but really, I'm sorry. You didn't know what you were getting into when you agreed to the bet."

I slowly make my way over to her and drop to my knees, spreading her legs wide so I can shift between them and rest my hands on her thighs. "I had some idea. Your family is kind of notorious for being hard asses."

Her beautiful lips curl into a smile, and I reach out and brush a finger over them.

"And after everything you told me over the course of the last week, I kind of figured the situation was going to be tense."

She lets out another little sigh that flutters the hair around her face. "Still…my mother insulted you."

I chuckle and lean in to press my lips against hers softly. "Stop apologizing for your mother. I'm a big boy, and I can stand up for myself when a situation calls for it."

And that wasn't one where I needed to say a word. Anything I would have attempted to say to disperse the tension would have only succeeded in making it worse. Sometimes knowing when to say nothing is just as important as knowing what to say.

Athena wraps her arms around my neck and drags me

closer until her breasts press into my chest. Her tongue slides out along my lips, requesting entrance, and we sink into a kiss far more intense than any one we've shared before. Her groan vibrates against my lips, and she shifts her body, pushing her core against my stomach.

I drag my mouth away and capture her face between my palms, and her lust-soaked eyes meet mine. "What are you doing, Princess?"

One corner of her mouth tilts up slightly. "That should be obvious."

It would be if this were anyone but Athena Warren or if we had met under any other circumstances.

"Princess…"

She shifts forward and tightens her grip on my neck, lowering her forehead to press it against mine. "Please, Isaiah. There's only one thing I want right now. One thing that will make everything okay for a while."

"Jesus, Princess…"

Her words cut straight to my core, directly to the part of me that wants to be the one who gives her pleasure and makes her smile, makes her life a little bit better, and gives her everything she deserves.

The part of me that I don't think I can ignore.

CHAPTER 15

ISAIAH

"You're sure, Princess?"

She responds by slamming her lips to mine again and pulling me toward her as she falls back onto the couch again. Her soft body presses to mine, and a low groan climbs up my throat and into her mouth when she opens for me to slip my tongue inside.

Athena may be young, but she's also a woman who knows what she wants. In this moment, we clearly want the same thing. Whatever this is between us has been slowly building since the moment she slid into that chair across from me at the bar in Berkeley.

We've developed the kind of connection I never thought I would feel with another human being, let alone in such a short amount of time. And now, we'll be able to come together in the way I've only fantasized about.

Over and over and over again.

Reluctantly, I drag my head back from hers. She offers a

little gasp of dismay, but I grasp the hem of her shirt, and she sits up to let me pull it up and off her.

I let it fall to the floor without a care about where it lands, my focus only on the beauty in front of me.

Her flawless, creamy skin practically glows under the overhead light, her breasts pushed up by the lacy black bra. She reaches behind her to undo the clasp, and I slip my fingers under the straps and drag them slowly down her arms to let it fall to the floor with her shirt.

"Christ, Athena. You're fucking beautiful."

My palms burn to touch her, to feel her under me, but I hesitate again. She leans forward slightly, almost offering herself up to me. Any reservations I have disappear instantly. I'll take that invitation any day.

I brush my thumb over one of her pert nipples, and she gasps, her eyes rolling back in her head. She rolls her hips against my jean-encased cock, seeking friction and relief.

She can't possibly know what she's doing to me, how incredibly flawless she is.

I'm completely lost to this woman.

Capturing her lips with mine, I toy with her nipples, brushing and twisting and tweaking them until she is practically humping me, hovering on the edge of release. But I don't want to make her come this way. I want to be touching her, tasting her.

I slowly run my hands down the smooth expanse of her stomach to the button of her jeans and pop it open. Her lips seek mine desperately, and I urge her to raise her hips so I can slide off her jeans and panties. She breaks away and pants, watching me with hooded eyes, assessing my every move.

We've seen glimpses of each other undressing, have been almost naked together in a hot tub. But this is different.

So much different.

I grasp the hem of my shirt and pull it off, then move to free my aching cock from the confines of my jeans. Her eyes follow my hands eagerly, and I push to my feet to shove down my pants along my boxers, all under the watchful gaze of the woman who seems intent on testing my resolve.

Her eyes zero in my length, and her tongue slides out along her lips.

Damn...

Stroking myself slowly, I lower myself back onto my knees in front of her. "Don't look at me like that, Athena. I need to make this last."

She raises her eyebrow at me as if in question, but she doesn't say anything. Her bare pussy glistens under the overhead light, wet with her arousal, and I reach out with my free hand and drag my thumb along the seam and over her clit.

"Oh, God!" Her eyes roll to the back of her head again, and her hips fly up wildly at the contact.

I lean over her and capture her tiny gasps with my kiss as I roll my thumb around her most sensitive place. "You're so wet and ready for me, Princess, but I'm going to make you come before I do. Way more than once."

She groans in response, and I stroke myself with one hand and slip two fingers inside her. Her mouth falls open on a strangled gasp, and she clenches against my digits.

"Isaiah…"

My name falling from her lips while she orgasms and clasps around my fingers is like a flare setting my body on fire.

"God, you're beautiful, Athena." I kiss her deeply, feeling the little shocks and quivers roll through her body. "But we aren't done, Princess. Not even close."

Shifting back a little, I urge her legs open more and settle into the perfect position. She pushes up and watches me, her brow furrowing slightly, and I dip my head and run my tongue straight through her glistening lips, never looking away from her.

Athena gasps again and reaches up to run her fingers through my hair, clinging to me like I am her lifeline while I bury my face between her legs and devour her.

The taste of her orgasm seeps onto my tongue, and a groan of satisfaction rumbles deep in my chest.

Athena Warren is every bit as incredible as I imagined, and seeing her come undone because of me only makes me want to do it again and again until she's nothing but a boneless, quivering mass, the stresses and tension of the day long forgotten.

Her hips roll up to meet me, her hands tightening on the back of my head. "Oh, God, Isaiah."

I slip two fingers inside her and curl them, setting a rhythm with them and my tongue designed to make her come hard and fast. Her orgasm finally hits her, and she jerks and vibrates, gripping me like a vise and finally shifting away when she can no longer handle the intensity of the contact.

So damn beautiful.

I draw back and lick my lips as I settle between her legs. She doesn't look away, just watches as I brush the head of my cock against her core. A shudder rolls through her, and she wraps her arms around my back, her lips a mere hairsbreadth from mine.

"Please, Isaiah. Do it."

"Hell, Athena. I want to, but I need to get a condom first."

She shakes her head and holds on to me so I can't pull away. "I'm clean and on birth control."

Shit. Bareback inside Athena, I'll last about five seconds.

"I haven't been with anybody in a long time, and our company insurance requires we get tested every six months. I'm clean. But we really should still—"

"No." She presses her lips to mine gently. "I want to feel you—all of you."

Sweet hell.

I nudge the head of my cock between her legs and align, entering her slowly.

Her eyes widen, and she gasps out a breath. "Oh, God, this is what it feels like."

"What?"

ATHENA

Isaiah freezes with his cock halfway inside me, his entire body going rigid, and he pulls his head back slightly to look at me straight-on.

Crap.

I hadn't meant to say anything. Didn't want him to know. But it felt so good. I couldn't control my tongue. The words just fell away the same way any reservations did.

His hard green gaze locks with mine. "Athena…are you… a virgin?"

The quiver in his usually strong voice makes me dart my gaze from his when I say the word, unable to look him in the eye even while we're still connected like this. Because I know it will change things between us and might be the end of *this.*

"Yes."

"What? How is that even possible?" He starts to pull away, but I drag him back toward me with a firm grip on his shoulders.

"Don't stop. Please. I want this." As if to prove my point, I clench around his cock, still partially inside me, and he groans and squeezes his eyes closed. "I want to be with you, Isaiah."

For the first time in my life, I'm finally with someone I feel is deserving of this, who I want to share it with after what we've been through together.

Slowly, he opens his eyes and stares at me as if he's waiting for me to change my mind.

I'm not going to. This entire trip has been drawing us closer and closer, and I want my first time to be with him. With someone I care about and not just some thick-headed frat boy who wants to get laid.

"Please…" I roll my hips, bringing him in even deeper.

He takes my face between his palms and brushes his lips against mine. It's reverent and careful, not at all the impassioned kisses of only moments ago. "Are you sure, Princess? You don't have to do this. We can stop."

Something dark flickers in his gaze, a moment of hesitation, almost like he wants me to put an end to what is about to happen, but I nod and urge him with my feet again, and he pushes fully into me, stretching me and filling places I didn't know needed him so badly.

"Oh!" Anything else I might say falls away at the sensation of having him inside me. Of finally doing this. With *him.*

Isaiah presses his lips to my cheek, a heavy pant in my ear. "Tell me if I'm going too hard or too fast."

I nod, and he withdraws slowly, then plunges back in, rolling his hips to grind against my hypersensitive clit. Squeezing my eyes closed, I clench around him instinctively.

Even though I came twice before he got inside me, I'm already poised to blow again, and it's nothing like it is when I touch myself. It's so much better. So much deeper. It's so damn obvious why people love doing this so much.

I thought your first time was supposed to hurt, supposed to be uncomfortable, but it's far from that with Isaiah. We move naturally, rising and falling, cresting in perfect unity. I have no idea what I'm supposed to be doing right now, but my body seems to have a mind of its own. Seems to know what I need and how to get it from him.

I roll my hips up to meet every one of his slow thrusts, every fiber of my being pulsing and coiling, needing more, wanting more. "Harder."

He kisses me deeply, his tongue probing my mouth as he increases his pace infinitesimally. I wrap my legs around his back and dig my heels into his ass, urging him on, searching for what I can see just beyond my reach on the horizon.

Isaiah thinks I'm going to break, that I'm some sort of delicate porcelain doll who can't handle it, but I would think that after what we did during our last week together, he would realize I'm stronger than I look.

He pulls back slightly and grasps my hips to angle them up slightly, which makes the head of his cock drag against someplace inside me that sends my head spinning and warmth flooding through all my limbs.

"Oh, right there."

A low groan rumbles in his chest, and he plunges into me a little harder, a little deeper, his pelvis rolling against my clit with each thrust until I finally can't take it anymore. My entire body seizes and goes rigid before the most mind-bending, earth-shattering orgasm of my entire existence rushes over me.

He keeps going, driving into me, his shoulders tense, muscles in his neck straining. And he's magnificent.

Isaiah is true masculine beauty. And he has a warm, genuine heart to go with it. He's the whole package, and at least for now, he's mine. He finally whispers my name and comes, stilling over me, his thrusts erratic. "Fuck."

He drops his forehead against mine, our heavy breaths mingling together. The only thing that exists in the moment is us.

But the spell is broken when he drags his head back and

his gaze meets mine. That same darkness lingers there, and he brushes his thumb over my lips. "I don't deserve you, Athena."

I run a hand back through his hair and manage to suck in enough air to get out my response. "The last week has been the best of my life. Thank you, Isaiah."

He buries his face against my neck and sags against me. An incredible man who just gave me the most incredible night of my life, despite how terrible parts of the day might have been.

What more could a girl ask for?

CHAPTER 16

ATHENA

"Are you sure you're ready for this?" Isaiah tugs on my hand to stop me at the bottom of the staircase.

I turn back toward him and offer him a half-smile I am not really feeling. "I can't avoid them forever." My stomach grumbles loudly, and I point to it. "Plus, it's time to eat, and my body knows it."

He inclines his head toward the front drive where we left his bike when we finally came back an hour ago with just enough time to clean up before dinner. "We could always hop back on the bike, drive around until we find a Chinese restaurant that's open, and grab some chow mein and beer instead of dealing with the family table drama."

I wrap my arms around his neck and pull him down to press a kiss to his lips. "As amazing as that sounds, I don't think I can get away with it. Thank you for the ride today, though. It was just what I needed to kind of reset before the big showdown."

He smirks at me and brushes my hair back to tuck it

behind my ear. "You're welcome. But that was kind of a selfish move on my part."

"Oh, yeah, how so?"

Isaiah presses his body against me and brushes his lips over mine. "Because I knew once we left that pool house this morning that I was going to miss having you so close and in my arms. I've become spoiled having you wrapped around me for six days."

I chuckle and shake my head. "Yeah. It does feel a little weird, doesn't it?"

He shrugs. "A little—"

"Oh, there you two are!"

I wince and pull back from him at the sound of Grandmother's voice floating through the foyer.

She hustles over to us and offers a kind smile before she winks at Isaiah. "We're just about to sit down for dinner."

The woman who always seems to have impeccably bad timing slides one arm through his and her other one through mine and ushers us toward the dining room.

She leans toward me and whispers conspiratorially. "Your mother and father seem to have cooled down a little bit since last night. I saw Artie and Archie talking to them this morning and things were relatively serene. Your grandfather, though..." She shakes her head and purses her lips. "Something has gotten to him, and I can't quite figure it out. So, keep your wits about you."

I snort and laugh, the sound echoing down the long hallway. "When do I ever not?"

"Very true, dear. I never have to worry about you standing up for yourself."

As we approach the dining room, she pauses and turns to Isaiah, patting his hand where it rests on her arm. "The Warrens can be a bit overwhelming, as you experienced a little of last night. Don't let it throw you off your game."

He chuckles and presses a kiss to her cheek. "Don't worry about me, Mrs. Warren. I got this."

"I'm sure you do, dear."

Grandmother seems completely unfazed by Isaiah's appearance with me yesterday or the fact that the big, burly biker in jeans, T-shirt, and a beard is crashing our family Thanksgiving dinner. She leads us through the archway and into the immaculately set dining room.

Father already sits at the head of the table with Grandfather on the opposing end, but there isn't any sign of Mother or the rest of the clan.

I turn to Grandmother. "Where is everyone else?"

"We were hiding, too." Artie's voice behind me makes me jump, and I whirl around to face him.

He stands just behind me, his arm around Penelope, who's holding Persephone, Max at his side. Archie and Blaire wait just behind them, knowing smirks on both their faces.

Artie wraps me up in a hug and kisses me on the cheek. "You doing okay today?"

I nod, and he steps forward to shake Isaiah's hand. "You must be Isaiah. Nice to meet you."

Isaiah grins. "You, too. I've heard a lot of good things."

Artie laughs and glances over his shoulder at me. "I bet."

He slaps Isaiah on the shoulder and ushers him farther into the dining room. Penelope gives me a quick half-hug, and I ruffle the hair on Max's head as he passes.

"Hey, buddy."

"Hi, Aunt Athena." He bounces along and hops into his chair between his mother and father, across from where Isaiah waits for me, watching expectantly.

Archie steps up and wraps me in a hug. "We have your back today. Nice call on bringing home the dirty biker." He chuckles and shakes his head as he pulls away. "You one-upped me there."

Blaire smacks him on the shoulder playfully. "Yeah, all you did was bring home your secretary." She steps forward and gives me a hug. "Good to see you, Athena."

"You, too."

Archie leans in as he passes. "But seriously, we have your back."

"I appreciate that more than you know."

He waggles his eyebrows and inclines his head toward Isaiah. "From the looks of it, the fake date doesn't seem so fake anymore."

Heat rushes to my cheeks and floods between my legs as I think about what happened last night...and again this morning. "Yeah, not so much anymore." I grin at Archie while trying to hide my body's natural response to discussing Isaiah.

"Good for you, little sister. You deserve to have some fun."

Fun...

It definitely has been. This week has been more than I ever could have imagined in so many ways.

I follow Archie into the dining room and take my seat next to Isaiah.

He leans toward me and glances at the empty seat next to Father. "Where's your mom?"

Shrugging, I reach forward for the glass of wine already poured for me that I'm sure I'm going to need. "Who knows?"

Almost as if on cue, Mother rushes in, her eyes widening slightly when she takes in everyone already around the table. "Oh, you're all here. I was just double-checking something with the cook."

She flutters over to her seat and lowers herself into it, her eyes immediately darting to narrow on Isaiah. Grandmother may be right that they've calmed down a bit, but that doesn't mean Bunny Warren has any plans to embrace my date with open arms.

Father pushes to his feet and grabs his wine glass. "May I propose a toast…"

Everyone grabs their glasses and raises them.

"To having the entire Warren family back together for this Thanksgiving." Father tips his glass toward Isaiah. "Along with our guest, Isaiah…" He raises his eyebrows, realizing he doesn't know his last name.

Isaiah clears his throat. "Wolfe. Isaiah Wolfe."

Father nods. "Thank you for getting Athena home on time."

"Yes, it certainly was nice of Mr. Wolfe to give her a ride home."

I freeze, and everyone turns to look at Grandfather. The old man barely says a word these days unless it's to criticize someone or put his foot down about something.

Father flits out his hand, dismissing the comment. "Anyway"—he lifts his glass again—"to the many things we have to be thankful for. Salute!"

"Salute!" Everyone takes a sip of their wine and sets down their glass except Isaiah beside me, who gulps down almost half of it.

I rest my hand on his thigh. "Are you okay?"

He gives me a forced smile that doesn't quite touch his eyes. "Yep, all good. Just thirsty."

Apparently.

The servers step in with the first course before any more awkwardness can occur around the table, and Isaiah rests his hand on my thigh and squeezes it gently.

He leans toward me and grins. "I have a lot to be thankful for this year."

I offer him what might be the first genuine smile I've ever given at this table. "Me, too."

ISAIAH

Artemis Warren—the first, the patriarch of the family—continues to eye me with a cold, icy glare from his spot at the end of the table. Even from this distance, it sends a chill through my spine.

You're reading too much into it.

I've been trying to convince myself of that since dinner started and avoid making eye contact with the old man, but every once in a while, that tingle of knowing his focus is on me drags my attention toward him, despite my best efforts to ignore it.

Like I'm trying to do now by returning my focus to the conversations at the table that I've zoned out from for the last half an hour as course after course has been placed in front of me.

Athena's grandmother chatters on with Blaire and Penelope easily while Artie, Archie, and their father discuss business near the far end of the table, leaving Athena's mother to sit with her lips twisted in a scowl, taking in all the chatter around but barely participating.

I lean over to Athena and wrap my arm around her shoulders to draw her closer to me. "Is your mother really always like this?"

She shrugs slightly and darts a quick peek at the woman who has been the source of most of her turmoil. "This is our first family holiday all together. She and Father took the Penelope and Max situation and Artie leaving the company hard, and then when Archie decided to marry Blaire, it was another blow. I think having all that shoved in their face at once might be too much for her."

I run a hand over my beard. "And maybe I was the final straw that broke the camel's back?"

She presses a kiss to my cheek. "Don't worry about it. She'll get over it. She always does."

Something tells me Bunny Warren doesn't really get over anything; she just holds all of her anger and resentment inside until it finally boils over.

"So, Isaiah…"

I turn toward Archie on my right.

"Athena told me about a couple stops you guys made. Which was your favorite?"

A tossup between the hot tub the first night and getting to finally kiss her in Hershey.

Neither of which I'm willing to share at this dinner table.

I clear my throat and pull away from Athena. "I really enjoyed the racetrack in Indianapolis. Even though we didn't have time to do the racing experience and drive or anything, it was still cool to do the tour and see where it all happens."

"I bet the racetrack has tight security, doesn't it?

My spine stiffens at Athena's grandfather's question.

First, the comment about my name, and now, this slight allusion to the family business.

I clear my throat and address him. "They sure did. With as expensive and dangerous as those cars are, they really need it."

He gives an imperceptible nod at my response, and Athena's grandmother leans and whispers something to him that makes his jaw harden.

Athena's mother watches everything with hard eyes but doesn't offer anything.

Archie turns to Artie. "We should go sometime. Maybe for the 500? What do you think, Max?"

The kid lights up and bounces in his seat. "Yeah! Yeah! Racecars!"

I smile at the simple joy he has. To be so young again and carefree, completely oblivious to how complicated the world can be, even sitting at this table.

Athena's mother takes a sip of her wine and sits back in her chair to allow one of the servers to remove her empty plate. "Athena, I assume you're going to be flying back since you don't have another week to flit about the United States on the back of the bike before you have to return for classes?"

Shit.

I wince on Athena's behalf, but she just forces a smile. "I would appreciate the use of the jet, Mother. I do need to get back for classes and finals."

Bunny Warren turns her laser focus on me. "And what about you, Mr. Wolfe? Will you be needing a ride on the family jet back to Berkeley, or are you just going to skip a week's worth of classes to give you time to get back on that motorcycle of yours?"

Athena stiffens next to me and reaches for her wineglass, which has already been refilled at least once.

We haven't discussed it again—what's going to happen come Sunday and the end of the weekend, the end of my agreement for losing our bet. But I can't go back to Berkeley, no matter how much I want to now that things have changed between Athena and me.

Father, James, and Jacob are expecting me home. Hell, they were expecting me home a week ago. I can't leave them hanging like this any longer.

"I actually have some family things to deal with before I can go back."

Bunny raises an eyebrow, and the tiniest of smirks tilts the corner of her lips.

Is the woman actually gloating, thinking that I'm going to be abandoning her daughter?

"So, when will you and Athena see each other, then?"

I reach under the table and grab Athena's hand, squeezing it gently to try to convey to her just how much I mean the words I'm about to say. "As soon as I can."

Bunny balks. "That sounds awfully vague."

This woman is itching for a fight, but I'm not about to start one with her at the dinner table, especially not when the old man may know what I'm hiding.

Instead, I force a smile at her. "It is, but we'll figure it out."

"It's a rather long distance to try to have a relationship, isn't it?" Artemis, the first's voice, breaks in, and he raises his bushy white eyebrow. "Boston to Berkeley. Almost as far apart as you can be in this country."

Shit.

I'm confident I never mentioned being from Boston to anyone other than Athena, who hasn't been out of my sight since we arrived, so it's unlikely she told anyone. That can only mean one thing...I'm screwed.

CHAPTER 17

ISAIAH

The final dessert plates get cleared from the table, and just in time. I'm not sure I could handle any more time sitting here under the scrutiny of the Warrens.

Athena is tougher than I even thought if this is them on their best behavior because they have a guest at dinner. The jibes her mother sent our way weren't even thinly veiled. They were direct shots designed to wound.

The only saving grace over the last two hours has been Archie and Artie and their wives, along with Ruby Warren. Athena mentioned her grandmother often butted in and set the other Warrens onto the right track, but she does it so subtly and with a tact Athena's mother seems to lack.

Despite how much the temperature has dropped since we got back from our ride earlier, I somehow doubt Athena will say no if I suggest we hop back on the bike and get the hell out of here for a while.

I follow her out of the dining room and grab her hand to

stop her from going up the stairs. The tension in her body since her mother's harsh words about what lies in our future makes the gourmet meal we just had sit heavy like lead in my stomach.

As much as I want to tell her the truth about why I'm not going back to Berkeley, the truth about our entire trip and how it came to be, I don't want to add to her distress when she's already dealing with her parents and grandfather this weekend. Come Sunday, we'll talk. Lay everything on the table and make a plan. Because I meant what I told her mother at that table—I want to see Athena again as soon as humanly possible.

And every day after that, if there's any way for us to make it work.

Athena turns to face me, her lips pressed into a firm line that mirrors her defensive stance. "What?"

"Let's go for a ride."

She opens her mouth to reply, but a deep voice from behind me and a firm hand on my shoulder interrupt her.

"Isaiah, join me in the study for an after-dinner drink."

Dammit.

Athena's grandfather isn't making an offer. It's a command from one of the most powerful men in the country. And the old man clearly has more on his mind than enjoying a nightcap with me.

I offer Athena an apologetic half-smile, and she inclines her head for me to go with her grandfather. She knows as well as I do that he is the type of man you can't say no to. But following him down the hallway toward the study feels a bit like a death row inmate walking to his execution.

Something tells me this isn't going to be a pleasant conversation, no matter how many fake smiles he may offer when others are around.

The old man holds the door for me, then nudges it shut after I step into the opulent study. The room is filled with overstuffed leather furniture, heavy, dark wood bookcases, and the smell of old booze and good cigars.

He offers me a hard smile that contains no warmth before he makes his way over to the bar on the far side of the room and pours two tumblers of expensive scotch. "I thought it would be appropriate for you and me to chat in private, Mr. Wolfe." He crosses the room back to me and hands me one of the drinks. "Or should I call you Mr. Frost?"

Shit.

I down a massive gulp of the smoky scotch, letting it burn my throat as I tighten my hand around the crystal tumbler. "Why don't we just go with Isaiah?"

The man at the helm of one of the most powerful families in America settles back in one of the huge leather armchairs and crosses his ankle over his knee, watching me closely. It may appear to be a relaxed position, but I know better—it's all an act. The eldest Artemis Warren was one of the best litigators this country has ever seen, and then he ruled from his position on the Supreme Court for decades before he finally retired recently after having a heart attack and other health issues.

He's an expert at cross-examination and will use it to get all the information he wants—and he clearly wants something from me.

Likely an explanation. "I appreciate you not saying anything at dinner."

It was clear almost from the beginning that he knew or at least suspected who I was, but he didn't call me out in front of Athena like he could have—likely for a good reason.

He takes a sip of his drink and grins at me. "I figured there was an explanation for why you weren't offering up a lot of personal information. And it seems pretty clear that my granddaughter doesn't know who you really are."

I rub at the back of my neck with my free hand. "Not exactly."

"So, you're lying to her?"

Shit.

"No. It's nothing like that. I was going to tell her...on Sunday. When all this"—I wave a hand around—"settles a little bit."

The old man chuckles and takes another sip of his drink. "Nothing ever really settles around here."

"That isn't a surprise. But really, sir, I'm not trying to lie to her. I just wanted to give her a week of not having to worry about anything or questioning motives. Some time to just relax before she got here and had to deal with her mother trying to set her up and control her life."

It may not have been the wisest statement to make, and he certainly could take offense to the characterization of his daughter-in-law, but being honest seems to be the best play right now.

But instead of getting angry, he just nods slowly and rolls his glass between his hands. "Does your father know you here?"

I shake my head. "No, and I'd like to keep it that way."

He smirks. "I'm sure you would. I've known him for many years, you know? Your mother, too. I thought you looked familiar last night when you rode up with my granddaughter on your bike. The beard made it a little hard to see initially, but now, looking at you, I don't know how I missed it last night." He inclines his drink toward me. "You look like him. Or like he did thirty years ago."

"I guess I'll take that as a compliment."

"As soon as I heard the last name Wolfe, I knew for sure. Using your mother's maiden name probably would've worked with anyone else, but I've known both families for a very long time."

Just my luck...

I take another sip of my drink to try to quell the growing tightness in my chest. "Again, I appreciate you not saying anything."

"I wanted to get the lay of the land and figure out what was going on before I had a discussion with my grand-daughter. I don't like her being lied to, and I have to wonder what a billionaire heir to one of the largest and most successful private security firms in the world is doing riding across the country on a motorcycle with a twenty-one-year-old college senior on the back, seemingly clueless."

That's a fair question considering the circumstances, and I open my mouth to answer when the hinges of the door behind me squeak.

Oh, God. No.

I turn to find my worst nightmare standing in the jamb, tears shimmering in the eyes that looked at me with so much affection such a short time ago.

ATHENA

The food I just ate and wine I just drank to try to keep my cool during dinner attempt to make a reappearance as I stare at the man I gave my heart and body to, the one who I apparently don't know at all.

Clenching my fists at my sides, I swallow through the emotion threatening to choke me. "Who are you? Really? Not Prez272? Do you even go to Berkeley?"

"Shit." He runs a hand back through his hair and sets his

drink on a table before he approaches me, his entire body tense, brow furrowed.

Oh, God...

The fact that he didn't immediately respond slams to the forefront of my mind. I back away a step. "Jesus. You don't. What the hell is going on?" I look over his shoulder at Grandfather. "I heard what you said about his family. Was this all some setup?"

The thought turns my stomach again, but I swallow the bile rising in my throat and glare from Isaiah to the man who has always controlled everything in this family, almost silently directing things like some mysterious conductor hiding in the shadows.

"Was this all some ploy to bring an appropriate guy into my life in hopes that it would somehow make me fall in line before I graduated?"

It would be typical Warren behavior. Mother and Father had a hand in trying to keep Artie from Penelope all those years ago, and when Archie announced he was marrying Blaire last New Year's Eve instead of someone they approved of, their response almost cost them their relationship with him, too.

I wouldn't put it past them to send Isaiah *Frost* to Berkeley to try to woo me in order to ensure I married properly and returned to the East Coast to live what *they* deem to be an appropriate life.

Grandfather slowly climbs to his feet. "I had nothing to do with this. We all have our thoughts about your future plans, but I would never interfere this way."

Despite how invasively he and Mother and Father *have* interfered where Artemis and Archimedes are concerned, I actually believe him. He appears as surprised by Isaiah being here with me as I am by learning who he really is.

He lied to me.

About his name. About why he was in Berkeley. About his last *name*.

How can I believe anything he said?

I suck in a shaky breath, but it doesn't stop the room from spinning. Each breath gets harder and harder to pull in. Tears sting my eyes, but I refuse to let them fall; I refuse to give Isaiah that satisfaction.

Instead, I level my gaze on him. "Well, if *he* didn't set this up, did you? Was this all just some game to see if you could land the Warren heir?"

Isaiah has the balls to look offended by my question after everything he's done. "Jesus, Athena…no, of course—"

I hold up a hand to stop him. "Don't say *of course* like I'm just supposed to accept you at your word. I don't want to hear any more lies."

"Athena, please, let me explain."

Squeezing my eyes closed, I shake my head. I can't even bear to look into the eyes of the man who offered me so much joy over the last week. Not when all of it was a lie.

My entire body starts to vibrate, and I open my eyes to find Isaiah has closed the distance between us.

He stands right in front of me now and extends a hand. "Athena, please, just five minutes so I can explain."

"There isn't any explanation necessary. You're no better than them." I motion toward where we just had our very awkward dinner. "All you see are ways to manipulate people for your own gain. And I was the dumb, naïve girl who fell for it."

I turn away from him and rush out of the study as fast as my feet and my anger can carry me. Heavy footsteps follow in my trail, but I don't look back. My chest constricts so tightly that I can't even breathe, each breath a struggle as I race toward the front door.

Loud chatter coming from the living room up ahead to

the right means there won't be any way for me to get outside without the rest of the Warrens seeing me, but I can't worry about that or what they will think right now. If I don't get some cool fresh air soon, the blackness encroaching on the edges of my vision may completely takeover and I might pass out.

The closer I move toward the door, the louder the voices become, and Father and Mother step out from the living room, after-dinner drinks in their hands, just in time to see me barrel past them.

Mother raises her eyebrows, something that almost passes as genuine concern crossing her face. "Athena, what's going on?"

Isaiah's heavy footsteps close in on me. "Athena, wait!"

Father's booming voice echoes through the vaulted foyer, "Isaiah, what's wrong?"

"I'll talk to her."

Crap.

He's directly behind me now, so close I can practically feel every breath that liar takes against the back of my neck. Only hours ago, that might have been comforting, something I longed for, but now, it just makes me want to run harder.

And freedom is in sight.

I grab the door handle and jerk it open, stepping into the cool November night air and scrambling across the driveway and out onto the perfectly manicured lawn.

Somehow, I thought this would help. Drawing in the chilly autumn air. Filling my lungs with that instead of the heady leather and man smell Isaiah seems to exude.

But it isn't any better out here. The pain in my chest only gets worse, like someone has ripped my heart straight out of it and left me bleeding out.

"Athena, let me explain."

I whirl around to face him, and the jerk actually has the nerve to look as upset as I feel.

How dare he?

"No." I point to his bike parked at the edge of the circular drive. "The only thing I want is for you to get back on that stupid bike and get the hell out of here."

CHAPTER 18

ISAIAH

Athena's words strike me harder than any of the semis
we passed on the highway during our trip ever could
have. The thought of riding off on my bike without her
wrapped around me makes my breath catch in my throat.
We've been so close for what feels like so long. And now, she
wants me to just go.

Don't leave like this.

I can't just turn my back on Athena and drive away as if
nothing happened between us—as if we didn't share something *deep* and *meaningful* and *real*. Not until I get a chance to
explain everything to her, to make her understand it and why
I made the choices I did.

It may not be enough. She may still never want to see me
or speak to me again. I couldn't really blame her for that. But
I at least have to *try* before I go back to Boston.

I slowly take a step toward her with my hands raised in
hopes she'll give me enough time to speak my piece. Another
step brings me close enough to reach out and touch her, and

she takes a little half step back, clearly ready to bolt if I keep advancing.

"If that's really what you want, Athena, I'll leave. But not until I explain."

She doesn't back away farther, but she eyes me warily.

It's the only opportunity she's going to give me to talk, so I need to seize it now.

"What your grandfather said is true. My family owns a large private security firm—Frost Security. My father—not me—has made a lot of money doing it. I work for the company in the corporate offices, helping him run things. When he retires, it'll get passed on to me and then to my brothers. So, yes"—I wave a hand toward the house—"I know what this life can be like. How much pressure it can put on you. Which is exactly why, after not taking a vacation for years, I jumped on my bike to travel across the country alone."

I needed that break from the phone calls and the meetings and staring at contracts until my eyes practically bled. And that trip west had been so relaxing. So good for my soul. It was exactly what I needed and had left me feeling rejuvenated in a way I had prayed for but hadn't really expected.

But then I met Athena, and everything changed.

For the better.

The way she looked when she walked into the door of Whiskey Jack's that night flashes through my head as if it happened yesterday. Her dark hair swinging around her face, blue eyes assessing me with a wiseness beyond her years.

It was how it all started. And now, everything has gone to shit.

"I only stopped in Berkeley to eat and grab a drink, and then, I was supposed to drive to LA that night and make arrangements to ship my bike and fly back to Boston." I pause for a second to give her time to process before I continue—and also a moment to bite back the anger thinking about what I'm going to tell her next brings up. "And there was this guy, well this group of guys, in the bathroom at the bar. He said you were meeting him there…"

Her eyes widen. Her spine stiffens, but she doesn't say anything, just watches me expectantly with a gaze filled with unshed tears.

I suck in a deep breath of cool air to prepare myself for her reaction to what I'm about to reveal—what I should have told her from the very beginning to avoid this exact situation. "He was bragging to his friends about things he was going to do to you on the trip, Athena."

She winces, and as much as I want to reach out and pull her into my arms to comfort her, I know it will only make things worse if I touch her right now. The last thing she wants in this moment is my touch. She doesn't trust me, and she may never trust me again.

"I wasn't sure what to do with that information." I shake my head, remembering how I turned over the options in my head that night. "Obviously, I recognized your name since our families somewhat run in the same circles. But we had never met. I didn't know you, and you didn't know me from Adam. I would've been a complete stranger walking up to tell you about that douchebag's plan. You had no reason to believe me any more than you did to trust him to give you a ride home safely. I could have been some jerk trying to get in your pants by telling you some lame story and being your savior. So, when you walked in—"

"You pretended to be Prez272."

I nod slowly. "I thought about telling you the truth about what I heard, but I didn't think you'd believe me. And I was worried that you'd go with him anyway, or worse, jump into a car with someone who might do something even more deplorable."

A multitude of horrific possibilities has played through my mind since that night, each worse than the last. My little lie to keep her safe seemed like the least of all the potential evils in those moments. But now, seeing how much I hurt her, how devastated she is, I may be wrong.

She scoffs, anger reddening her cheeks despite the chill outside where we stand on the lawn, and she fists her hands at her sides. "So, instead of telling me the truth, you just decided to seduce me yourself?"

ATHENA

Isaiah recoils almost as if I had physically slapped him.

His eyes widen, and he shakes his head. "No. God no. I didn't expect any of this to happen, Athena. I never wanted it to. I just wanted to get you home safely and have a good time." He runs a hand through his disheveled dark hair. "But then things changed between us, in a way I never expected. I just didn't know what to do."

He didn't know what to do?

Those words burn through my veins like a raging inferno, going straight to the part that the Warrens have always thought they could control through threats and manipulation. "How about telling me the truth from the beginning? Not treat me like some child who couldn't handle the truth."

He squeezes his eyes shut and shakes his head, rubbing at his temples like doing so will somehow change the decisions he made. "I know. I realize that now, and I never wanted you to find out this way."

"So, what? You were going to hide it from me forever? Pretend to be someone else?"

His eyes fly open, the deep green almost black in the

darkness of the evening. "Of course not. I had planned to tell you Sunday when it was time for me to leave and go back to Boston. I was going to explain everything to you and get you to forgive me…and tell you I love you."

I freeze, his words sinking into my already chilled skin. No one other than members of the family have ever said those words to me, and after all that's happened, I can't believe it coming from his mouth.

"I want you to go, Isaiah. Don't ever call me, don't show up again. If I see you at Berkeley, I'll hire security to ensure you stay far away." I snort at the irony of that statement and the fact that I might need to protect myself from the man whose family has made billions providing security for other people—the man whose arms I felt safer in over the last week than I ever have anywhere or with anyone else in my entire life.

How did it come to this?

Every flirtatious comment, every brush of a hand, every time I wrapped my body around his flashes through my head in an endless stream of memories I wish I could erase completely from my mind. "Just go, Isaiah."

He raises his hands again, pressing them together as if in prayer. "Please, Athena, just give me a chance—"

"You heard her." Mother's shrill voice cuts through the night air like a foghorn, and she steps out onto the lawn in her Louboutins and perfectly tailored dress, anger flaring pink on her cheeks. "My daughter told you to leave, and I want you off my property immediately, or I'll call the police."

It takes my mind a minute to process what just happened. Mother steps up next to me and wraps her arm around my shoulders protectively.

"If you so much as come within a hundred yards of Athena again, there's nothing your father or your connections will be able to do to save you from what I will unleash upon you."

Holy hell.

Bunny Warren has thrown the full force of the family name and her fury at Isaiah in my defense.

Father joins us on the grass and takes up a position on my other side. He glances between Isaiah and me before finally settling his focus on the man I never want to see again. "I suggest you go. Now."

Mother lifts her nose at him. "I'll have whatever belongings you left in the house mailed to your home in Boston. I don't want you setting foot in my house again."

Isaiah backs away, his eyes shimmering under the moonlight with unshed tears as hot, wild ones roll down my cheeks. I swipe them away quickly, but not before he sees them. If things were different, if they were anything like they had been only hours ago, he would reach up and brush them off my cheeks before kissing me and pulling me into his arms to offer whatever comfort he could.

Things changed so fast.

He looks so defeated, his shoulders sagging, but I'm the one who was lied to. I'm the one who got played by the one person I thought would never do that to me. This is my agony to feel, not his.

The fact that he's acting like it is only fuels my anger as I watch him walk away toward his bike. He pauses when he reaches it and turns back to look at me one final time before throwing his leg over the machine that brought us together. The engine roars to life, and my heart seems to fall into the rhythm, somehow still managing to beat despite feeling like it's completely shattered.

Mother tightens her arm around my shoulders, and as he pulls down the circular driveway, my gaze drifts to the open front door and the rest of the Warrens standing, watching all the drama unfold.

So much for a calm family holiday.

It's impossible for the Warrens. I don't know why I thought this would be any different or that things would go smoothly.

I poked the bear by bringing home a man who was literally a stranger to Thanksgiving dinner just to mess with Mother. And it was my turn to suffer the consequences of my actions.

Artie did.

Archie did.

They both came out okay on the other side—after a lot of turmoil and tears.

Maybe I will, too, some day. But right now, I only know one thing: I never want to see Isaiah Wolfe…*Frost…*again.

CHAPTER 19

THREE WEEKS LATER...

ISAIAH

"I just need to see her again."

James groans and pushes up from his seat on the couch in my office to make his way over to where I sit behind my desk. He walks around the hulking piece of wood furniture and smacks me upside the head.

My head jerks forward, and I turn and glare at him. "Ouch! What the hell?"

"Sorry, bro, but you deserve it."

Jacob chuckles from where he sits in an armchair facing me, his feet propped up on my desk. "He's right. You do. You need to stop talking about this girl. Need to stop thinking about her, too. You've been back for...what? Three weeks? And all you've done is whine about how much you miss her and how you need another chance."

I issue a low growl of warning at the twins. "Well, I'm sorry neither of you two assholes has ever been in love and can't possibly understand."

James barks out a laugh and sits on the edge of the desk.

"I'm pretty sure I'm in love with the blonde I brought home from the club last night."

He wiggles his eyebrows suggestively, and Jacob raises his hand for a fist bump.

"She was pretty hot."

"You two are disgusting."

Jacob raises an eyebrow at me. "Excuse me, but we aren't the ones who lied to a girl and got her to travel across the country with us and sleep in the same hotel rooms under false pretenses."

I sit up straighter, squaring my shoulders. "Hey, that's not fair."

"Isn't that what happened?"

Scowling at Jacob, I drop back into the chair. We have been over and over this a hundred times since I came back, and they're never going to let me hear the end of it.

"Will you two stop giving Isaiah so much shit and get back to work?"

We all turn toward the door where Dad leans against the jamb, his arms crossed over his chest.

"Yeah, yeah, yeah." James waves a hand dismissively. "We were just on our way back to our offices but stopped in to ask Isaiah about the contract with Drakeston."

One of Dad's white eyebrows wings up. "Is there some sort of problem?"

Jacob and James make their way toward the door, and Jacob smacks him on the shoulder.

"Nothing's wrong. Just need to clarify something. We did our work in nailing down that contract while big brother was driving across the country and picking up random college students."

I flip them off and watch them disappear into the hallway, still yucking it up. Dad closes the door and makes his way to settle in the chair Jacob just vacated.

"No word from her?"

Sighing, I rub my tired eyes. I haven't gotten a single night of good sleep since I got home, and it's hard to imagine that I ever will until I fix things with Athena. "No. I left messages on her cell phone, but either she changed her number, or she's deleting them without listening to them."

"Or maybe she's listening to them and just doesn't want to talk to you."

"Gee, thanks, Dad."

He chuckles lightly and shrugs. "I'm sorry, son, but I'm trying to be a realist here. When I messed up with your mom, I never knew how long it was going to take her to forgive me. But I always knew that she would eventually. Though, we were married for almost forty years before the Lord took her, so maybe I got more leeway…because God knows, I've made my fair share of stupid, unforgivable mistakes."

"And that is what I did? Something unforgivable?"

He barks out a laugh and shakes his head. "Well, I can't say that."

"What can you say?"

Dad and I have talked about my situation ad nauseam over the last few weeks, but I always feel like there's some huge piece of wisdom sitting on the tip of his tongue that could change everything when I have nothing else.

He leans forward and rests his elbows on his knees. "I spoke with her grandfather today."

I jerk up straighter in my seat. "You did?"

He shrugs.

"Well, what did he say?"

"That Athena went back to school on Monday after Thanksgiving as if her entire world hadn't blown up and that while he understands why you did it, he also respects her decision not to want to see you."

I slam my fist against the desk, rattling the few items I keep on it. "Shit. I really messed up."

Dad leans back in his chair. "You really love this girl?"

Scrubbing my hands over my face, I groan. "I do."

"And you know this after spending a week with her where most of the time you were on a motorcycle and not talking? Are you sure this isn't just some sort of lust that's going to fade as time passes?"

It's a question I've considered myself, one I've even tried to convince myself is true because it's better than the alternative—that I might actually love her and never see her again.

"All I know is that I haven't had a good night's sleep since I left there. I haven't been able to stop thinking about her. The way I felt when I was with her."

"Then I suggest you figure out a way to tell her that."

I smack my palms against the desktop. "She won't talk to me, Dad. She won't return my calls, and she's all the way in California."

He offers me a smirk. "And we have an entire fleet of jets at your disposal, Isaiah."

"We also have clients and meetings and things to take care of, and she said she doesn't want to see me. I have to respect her wishes."

He nods and pushes to his feet. "You're right. Showing up there isn't a good idea, so try to think of another way."

"That's all I've been doing for the last three weeks."

He raps his knuckles against the top of my desk. "I have faith you'll figure it out, son. You always do."

I wish I believed that.

ATHENA

"Are you going to stare at your phone all day?"

I glance up at Valerie and scowl. "I don't know. Are you going to be up my ass about it all day?"

Valerie barks out a laugh, and I can't help but grin back at her even though I feel like I haven't wanted to smile or laugh for weeks. She drops onto the couch next to me and sets her stack of books on the coffee table next to my open one that I haven't even looked at in the hour I've been sitting here.

This study session for our last final has quickly gone downhill in terms of progress.

She leans over to glance at my phone. "Did he leave another message?"

I shake my head and stare at the two dozen messages in my voicemail box that I still can't bring myself to either listen to or delete. "No. Not since yesterday."

One of her eyebrows slowly wings up. "And why do you look so upset? I thought you wanted him to stop calling you?"

Sighing, I drop my head back onto the couch. "That is what I want. Sort of."

"Sort of? What does that even mean?"

"If I knew the answer, it wouldn't be *sort of*."

She chuckles and drops her head against my shoulder. "You're a mess."

"I know."

My phone rings in my hand, and I jerk my head up to look at the screen, then frown at the name that pops up. "It's my grandmother."

"You should probably take it."

"I probably should." The old woman will just keep calling if I don't. I accept the call and put the phone to my ear, dropping my head back again. "Hello, Grandmother."

"Athena...how are you, dear?"

"That's kind of a loaded question right now, Grandmother."

She sighs, and for some reason, the familiar sound reaching through the phone offers almost a hug, one that I relied on my entire life to offer a little brief moment of normality when things got crazy at the house. "Have you spoken with him?"

"No. But he's left a bunch of messages I haven't listened to."

"Are you going to, dear?"

"I don't know."

Lately, it feels like I don't know anything. All the things I thought I knew seem uncertain now.

"You're still coming home for the Christmas party, aren't you?"

I wince and glance at Valerie who is trying to eavesdrop since I typically put these calls on speakerphone. "I don't know yet. I don't think I can handle a Warren party right now."

"Your mother and father will be very disappointed if you aren't here." She pauses, a heavy silence hanging between us. "You know how upset they were at what Isaiah did and how worried they are about you being out there all by yourself."

"I know."

Mother's defense of me out on that lawn, both of them coming to stand beside me to ensure I was okay and that he left, was something I never expected in a million years. It almost renewed my faith in them as human beings and parents. Almost.

And they didn't say "I told you so" even once during the several days I was still there after Thanksgiving. No one rubbed it in my face that things had backfired so badly with Isaiah.

Artie and Archie seemed to think seeing me so distressed is what finally sent a shock to their systems strong enough to snap them out of interloping-parent mode and into defending, protective parent mode.

Whatever it was. I am thankful for it. I'm not sure what I would've done had they not come out and if Isaiah wouldn't have left willingly.

The party is important to them. To us. To all the Warrens. I owe it to them to at least make an appearance.

"I'll come to the party. I can't promise I'll stay the entire night. You know how those things are."

Grandma chuckles. "You can't hide in the bathroom from them this year, Athena. If you're there, I expect you to do your best to mingle and play your role."

I groan and glance at Valerie. "I think I'll bring Valerie to be my stand-in."

Valerie shakes her head. "Oh no, you don't. I already told you, one Warren party was enough, and that one I went to freshman year with you almost killed me."

"That's a bit of an exaggeration."

She shakes her head. "No, it isn't. I will be safely ensconced at home in San Francisco while you are rubbing elbows with the rich and powerful of the East Coast."

I squeeze my eyes shut. "What time are they sending the jet for me?"

Grandmother laughs. "That's my girl. I think it should arrive Thursday evening, but I'm sure your mother will contact you with the exact time."

"I have no doubt she will. I'll talk to you later."

"Oh, Athena…"

"Yes?"

"Your grandfather meant well, you know, by not calling him out at the table in front of everyone. He wanted to talk to him privately before he said anything."

I sigh at the same thing Grandfather told me once I went back into the house Thursday night. "I know."

"He's concerned that you're angry at him and will somehow hold it against him."

"I'm not angry at Grandfather. I'm angry with myself for falling for his lies."

"Were they all lies?"

That's the ultimate question. The one that prevents me from deleting or listening to the messages. The one that has kept me awake every night since he roared off on that bike.

"Give my best to Grandfather."

"I will, dear."

I end the call and glance at Valerie. "You sure you can't come?"

She chuckles and grabs her stack of books. "Nope. After my last exam on Wednesday, I'm going home. I may even go with Tackett and his band for part of their tour over Christmas break before the new semester starts."

I raise an eyebrow at her. "Oh, really?"

"We'll see." She shrugs. "I haven't decided anything yet."

"Just be careful."

She winks at me. "I'm not the one jumping onto the back of motorcycles with total strangers."

"Ouch. Harsh."

A grin plays on her lips, and we both burst into laughter.

"Have fun with your family. You can tell them I'm devastated I can't attend."

I bark out a laugh and shake my head. "I'm pretty sure my parents would know that's bullshit."

She shrugs. "Maybe. Maybe not. Either way, my absence would at least be something to talk about besides the elephant in the room named Isaiah Frost."

"I know."

I'm going to have to find a lot of things to occupy my

mind and my time when I'm back home; otherwise, all I'll be thinking about is heading out to the boathouse and what happened out there. Something I've already thought about practically every moment since I've been back here.

Another reason I can't listen to or delete these messages. Because if I hear his voice one more time, I might break completely.

CHAPTER 20

CHRISTMAS EVE

ATHENA

Another year, another flawless Christmas party.

The lights dance around The American Museum of Natural History, showcasing the rich, the powerful, the all-too-important, and beautiful people gathered to celebrate the holiday the same way they do every year—with a big bash paid for and hosted by the Warrens.

Everyone looks so happy in their expensive designer gowns and tuxes, wearing picture-perfect smiles.

They make me sick.

Watching people be happy while my heart is still torn to shreds makes me wish I had stayed back in Berkeley for the winter break, even if Val isn't going to be there. Being alone would be better than seeing everyone enjoying themselves while I can barely keep myself from bursting into tears.

I raise the crystal champagne flute to my lips and guzzle down my umpteenth glass of the sweet drink in a manner I'm certain would have Mother cringing in horror at my very unladylike public display.

Maybe Bunny has had it right all along. Don't marry for love because, in the end, that love comes back to bite you on the ass—with razor-sharp teeth. That's why she pushed Artemis and Archimedes so hard, and it's why she's sought to steer me down her ordained path. But I can't possibly agree with Mother.

Maybe I am drunk, after all.

I just want to numb this endless, Isaiah-sized ache in my chest any way I can. If champagne can do it...keep them coming. It's better than the alternative—suffering through the party sober.

The band kicks up again, and Artie and Archie move to the dance floor with their wives, smiling and laughing, just living their best lives with the women they love. Those two seem not to have a care in the world because their worlds are safe within their arms.

I'll never have that. Not with Isaiah.

My chest tightens, and I grab another glass from the tray the passing waiter carries precariously.

While Mother and Father—and even Grandfather— finally got on board where Artie and Archie's marriages are concerned, after this Thanksgiving blow up, I bet Cliff Clifton is lurking around here in the shadows. No doubt Mother is waiting for the perfect time to spring him on me, like a big old husband trap.

Might as well bring him on. I lost my only shot at love.

"Maybe you should slow down a bit, Bud, save some for our guests."

I turn toward Father, looking every bit a Warren and the senator he is decked out in his impressive designer tuxedo. He hasn't called me Rosebud or Bud in years. If he's dragging out old nicknames, he must be gearing up to give me a huge lecture.

"You can spare me the lecture, Father. I've been beating myself up badly enough as it is."

I can't even meet his gaze, instead refocusing on the dance floor. The embarrassment of what happened still makes me cringe, and publicly licking your wounds isn't a Warren family trait.

Father doesn't say anything; he just leans against the railing with me and watches the revelry unfold down below. Just like Grandfather, he's a master litigator, and the silence acts as its own form of questioning worse than any lecture he could ever give. Disappointment pours off him in waves.

"I know I lied. I know I did something dangerous, and I know, in the end, my heart was broken. I get it. I deserve everything that's happened to me."

I take another shot of liquid courage.

Father slowly nods, finishes his scotch, and sets his glass on the tray of a passing waiter before turning to face me, a hip propped up against the railing. This is about as close to casual as I've ever seen the man in over twenty years on this Earth.

"Athena, your mother and I tried to raise you and the boys in a manner that would provide strong morals and work ethic. We have always held our children to higher standards because we didn't want a bunch of kids who had everything handed to them on a silver platter, but we also wanted to ensure your futures were secure. Now, I'm sorry that we persisted and pushed so hard when we thought we were making the best decisions for our children when clearly, we were not. I nearly lost my entire family because I've tried to control too much."

I cut my gaze to him, his words seeping under my skin and making my eyes burn with unshed tears. The last few years have aged him swiftly—heavy bags hang under his blue eyes, and the once salt-and-pepper hair has now become almost a full shock of white. Seeing my strong, proud father look so, well, sad makes a vise tighten around my chest.

He takes my hand in his, mindlessly stroking the back of it as if to comfort me. But I think it's more to comfort himself. "I missed years of my grandson's life that I'll never be able to get back because we didn't want Artie involved with Penelope. I'm done not being there in the way that my family needs me to be. Now, with that being said, my favorite daughter stands here devastated and all I want to do is hug her and help put the pieces of her broken heart back together."

Who is this man, and what has he done with Father?

I stare at him in stunned silence. "You want to hug me?"

It's been at least a decade, maybe longer, since this man has pulled me into his arms. The last time was probably when he had to pick me up from DeeDee Henderson's sleepover after we snuck and watched scary movies we weren't supposed to. To this day, they still give me the creeps. But back then, a hug from my old man made me feel better, safe. Since then, I've only experienced that with Isaiah.

"Of course, I do. If you'll let me." He holds out his arms, and without hesitation, I take a step into them.

An all-too-familiar smell that I've not been this close to in ages envelops me—crisp aftershave and a scent that is just Father's alone. Sighing, I settle into his embrace, resting my head against his chest. A couple of tears leak out onto his tux, and I soak up every ounce of comfort he's willing to give me.

"I'm crying on your tux." I softly laugh, but neither of us makes a move to release our embrace.

"Doesn't matter, Rosebud." He holds me a little bit tighter and pats me on the back. "I'm sorry I didn't do this more often. I'll regret some of my choices 'til the day I die. If you allow me to, I'd like to start making up for lost time."

Holy hell. It's a Christmas miracle!

I'm not certain what has caused this epiphany, but I won't question it. In fact, I welcome it. A vast change from the way things have run in the Warren house for as long as I can remember.

"I'd like that, Dad. I'd like that very much."

He squeezes me tighter before he holds me at arm's length, tears shimmering in his eyes. "Thank you for making this easy on an old man. I love you, Athena." He swipes a tear from his eye. "Your mother and your grandparents do, too, even though they're just as bad as I am with showing you sometimes."

An ache forms in the center of my chest at his words. It's not that I didn't know that. They care. That was never a question. They were always just so shitty at how they showed it. "I love you, too."

"Now, I must find your mother. I need to spin her around the dance floor. Will you be okay?"

"Yes, I'm fine. Go ahead. Go find Mother." I try to sound confident and lend reassurance to us both, but deep down, I'm a mess—and I don't see that changing anytime soon.

Father pats my arm and walks away to find Mother, and an almost peaceful calm settles over me now that I'm on new ground with him. It's a step in the right direction, even if the Warrens have a long way to go to heal the wounds of the past.

Again, I take my position at the railing, a new glass of champagne in hand. The party rages below, and I take it all in, a little less disgusted than I was before.

A familiar figure enters the room below, and the champagne flute almost slips from my hand. My breath stalls in my chest. My heart thunders against my ribcage, the glass trembling in my grip.

Isaiah. My Bikes. What is he doing here?

Tears fill my eyes for an entirely different reason now. The reality that even my own thoughts aren't true.

No, he is not your Bikes, Athena. Bikes was a fabrication. A figment of a bored man's imagination. None of it was real.

I try to turn away, to avoid looking at the man who destroyed me so completely, but I can't. All my eyes want to do is drink him in even when the rational part of me says to ignore him.

God, he looks amazing.

His dark, wavy hair slicked back from his forehead rather than disheveled from a motorcycle helmet and his clean-shaven face enhancing the angular features of his jaw—it's like he's a completely different man. If ever a body were meant to be in a tuxedo, it's Isaiah's. He fills it out so perfectly, and I'm positive his ass looks fantastic in the expensive, tailored material.

That asshole.

He grips a small, wrapped box in his hand and scans the room intently.

Looking for me.

There isn't any other reason he'd be here. The Frosts have never attended our party before that I know of, or if they did, I never noticed.

Those mossy-green eyes of his finally drift up to the balcony and meet mine. I can't stop the tears that slip down my cheeks no matter how hard I try. He focuses his gaze on me, and it's as if a quiver of arrows has been fired upon my already decimated heart.

A soft hand grips mine, catching me by surprise, and I turn to find Mother standing by my side.

"Mother?" My voice quivers. "What are you doing here? I thought you were dancing with Father?"

She offers me a not-unkind smile and squeezes my hand gently. "I thought you could use the support."

Bunny Warren coming to my rescue? AGAIN?

This night just keeps getting weirder, but I don't want her to think I don't appreciate her offer.

"Thank you, Mother. I'm okay, though."

Mother turns me toward her and wipes the tears from under my eyes with her free hand. She may have become stern and set in her ways over the years, but one thing hasn't changed—she's still the most beautiful woman in any room, and apparently, she has a few surprises up her sleeve.

"Of course, you are, Athena, darling. You're the strongest person I know."

"I don't feel very strong." I laugh, but it doesn't contain any humor, just frustration and anger toward the entire situation and the fact that he dared to show up here.

"Nonsense. You're a Warren." She pushes my hair off my shoulder, rearranging it back to perfection.

Her words and her touch are oddly comforting, almost like a warm blanket being wrapped around me. I inhale a deep breath and exhale slowly, regaining some composure.

"Do you want me to have him escorted out?"

She would do that very thing, personally, if I said yes. But I can't run from this and him forever. After the dozens of messages he's left, it's clear he isn't going to just stop without another conversation.

I squeeze her hand. "I'm okay. I'm a Warren."

Mother lightly kisses my cheek before giving me a wink and wordlessly floating away back into the party.

Either Hell has frozen over tonight, or both of my parents are losing their minds. Or maybe the spirit of this holiday season has finally worn through their tough outer shells. Whatever the reason, I'm not going to complain about this sudden shift in their demeanors. I'll just enjoy it—while it lasts.

Standing here amidst the shambles of my broken heart,

Mother just gave me the best Christmas gift—the strength to confront the man who broke it.

ISAIAH

My gaze automatically drifts upward, as if something is drawing me there instead of anywhere else in the vast space filled with revelers. Those blue eyes I've longed to see for so long stare back at me, shimmering with tears, her black hair perfect and sleek around her beautiful face.

She's stunning.

Then again, she always is, so it doesn't surprise me. What does is that after a whole month, just seeing her is all I need to make it feel like I can take a real, true breath again.

Athena is the oxygen I need to survive, the balm to soothe my aching soul, and she doesn't even know it if the way she's staring at me is any indication.

If I had any doubts before—which really, I didn't—I've confirmed it now; I'm crazy about that woman. A stark-raving-mad lunatic who only has one goal in mind—to do anything and everything I can do to show her how sorry I am, to prove to her I'm a man she can absolutely depend upon; a man she can trust; a man worthy of her love. Because life without her has been unbearable, even worse than how I felt before I took my cross-country trip.

Then, I was overworked and overstressed. Ready to break. Now, I'm broken because of what I did to that woman, because of the look of utter misery on Athena's beautiful face and knowing I put it there.

Absently, I reach up and rub at the ache in the center of my chest with my free hand while I try to gather enough courage to go up. Athena's mother approaches her and takes her hand. Given everything Athena told me on our journey and what I witnessed at that table on Thanksgiving, I doubt that's something that has happened often in the recent past. Though Bunny stood her ground next to her daughter that night, and from what I can see from my vantage point below them, it seems they've formed some sort of camaraderie in the last month. That's good because Athena needs someone by her side through all this.

James and Jacob may be dicks at times, but at the end of the day, they and Dad support me one hundred percent in any way they can. Athena never felt like she had that from anyone except maybe her brothers. To see the way she's interacting with her mother now gives me a little hope for the future of the Warrens, even if not for Athena with me.

Bunny Warren wipes tears from Athena's face, and knowing I'm the reason for them is like a punch to the gut. Coming here tonight was a big risk. One I maybe shouldn't have taken. This could ruin the entire party for Athena and her family, but I had to try. I had to take the chance to talk to her when I *knew* she would be here and have to hear me out.

Hopefully.

I inhale another deep breath and approach the stairs that will carry me to my princess. She watches me ascend, looking more like a queen awaiting an audience than a princess.

"Hello." My voice comes out shaky and uncertain, my nerves shot no matter how I might try and steady them.

The hand holding the small gift for her shakes so badly, I grip the box with both to try to prevent her from seeing what a wreck I am. Because the last month has been hell on me, and no doubt, looking into her eyes, it's been hell on her. I'll never forgive myself for hurting her, for putting her in a position to question her judgment and feelings for me and mine for her.

I'm such an idiot.

For weeks, I've dodged meetings and lain in bed like a lump of sad shit—as James would say. And he's right. I should have been doing everything within my power to fix things between us, but I also wanted to respect her wishes. She said she never wanted to see me or speak to me again. I didn't want to be a source of further consternation by continuing to call and leave messages she wouldn't respond to or by doing something even more brazen like flying across the country to see her in California. She had finals to prepare for and needed time to decompress and think about what went down.

I can't blame her. I deserve every bit of her anger. She felt betrayed because I did betray her by concealing the truth to try to protect her. She's a Warren, and I should have given her more credit.

"Hi." Athena's cool greeting settles over me, and it's so awkward. So uncomfortable. Things that just feel so wrong when it comes to this woman.

If it weren't for the people milling about and within earshot, I'd be hearing a lot of cuss words from her beautiful lips.

Rightfully so.

If I could kick my own ass, I would.

"Why are you here?" Her beautiful voice, once full of light and laughter that worked its way into my heart and soul, is now stony and cold, resolute that I'm the bad guy I made myself.

"I-I received an invitation." I raise an eyebrow. "I thought it was from you."

Did I have this all wrong?

Given the confusion twisting her lips, it appears the invitation didn't come from her.

My God, she didn't invite me?

"I'll leave. I'm sorry. I thought you invited me." I hang my head and turn to walk away, rubbing at that ache in my chest again, the one that has been there since the last time I had to drive away from this woman.

This time may kill me...

"Isaiah, wait..." She grabs my arm, stopping my momentum. I turn and take a lingering look into those blue eyes that haunt my every waking moment.

This will be the last time I see her.

I commit her every feature to memory. The color of her lips, the curve of her neck, the pain in her eyes that I put there. It's not how I want to remember her. I want to see her as that bright, funny, smart-ass girl who peed on the side of the road and told me off for laughing about it. The one who ate an entire seventy-two-ounce steak just to prove she could. The woman who begged me to be her first...

I don't deserve a moment more of her time.

Still, her hand tightens on my arm. "You came here tonight because you thought I wanted you here?"

She doesn't understand that I would do absolutely anything in my power to make her happy.

You broke her trust, you idiot.

That's the shittiest part of all. Maybe my intentions were good, but I withheld vital information. Information that may have altered her decisions had she known. I made her powerless, just like her family has done to her.

I'm a fucking asshole.

"Yes, of course, I came. Athena, I never meant to hurt you."

She lifts her hand between us to quiet me. Shutting up is the least I can do. She doesn't owe me anything, not even this conversation.

So, if she has something she wants to say, I need to let her.

"Just stop, Isaiah. We've been through this already. We

can't change what happened. You hurt me, you embarrassed me, but most of all, I trusted you. You, of all people, now that I know who you are"—she laughs, but there isn't any humor in it—"should understand how hard it is to trust someone in the world that we live in."

She isn't wrong. It isn't just hard; most of the time, it's damn near impossible, especially someone in her position with the power and glory of the Warren name.

"Had you looked like this when we met, clean-shaven, and impeccably dressed"—she waves a hand up and down my front—"I would have known from the start you're the very damn thing that I've been running from."

I expel a frustrated breath. No one else caused this clusterfuck but me. I need to fall on my sword. "I blew it. I'm sorry. I don't know what else I can say or do. Please, just tell me, whatever it is you want, whatever will fix this, and I'll make it up to you. I'll do anything to make this better."

Nothing changes in her stance or her gaze. No warming. No softening. Whatever happened between us on our trip, the true intimate moments I've clung to over the last month, I've tainted them all for her.

"Please, Athena…" My plea dies on my lips when Artemis and Archimedes step up next to Athena to protect their baby sister.

Artemis pokes a finger sternly into my chest, pushing me a step back from Athena and placing his frame between us. "What the hell are you doing here?"

I don't even bother replying to him. He isn't the most important person in this room. I peer over his shoulder at the woman who is still the center of my world, even if she doesn't believe it. "Athena, for what it's worth, I'm sorry."

She nudges at Artie's shoulder. "Just stay out of this, Artie. Isaiah was on his way out."

"Yeah, you better get your ass out." Archie points at me

over Artie's shoulder. "Do you need me to show you the door?"

Shit.

This tension isn't good for anyone, especially Athena. And I can't even blame her brothers for being mad. I'd be ready to beat my ass, too, if she were my sister.

I exhale a shaky breath, resigned to my fate because only I ruined us. I broke her heart. I put that look on her beautiful face and those tears in her eyes. I'm in love with Athena, and if setting her free is what it takes for her to be happy, I'll do just that, no matter how much it shatters me.

"Take care of yourself, Princess."

A tiny little sound slips from her lips at the use of my nickname for her, and she raises her hand to cover her mouth.

Turning to Artie, I press the gift into his hands. "Please give this to her."

He looks ready to argue for a moment, but apparently, concern over my getting the hell out of here takes over, and he raises a hand and points toward the door. I allow myself one last lingering look at her before I turn and head back down the stairs and toward the exit.

I don't glance back.

I can't.

If I do, I might change my mind and do something that makes things even worse for her. While I can't undo all I've done, she deserves to be at peace, something that won't happen with all that's taken place between us.

And her happiness is the most important thing in my world. So, I'll go. And I won't come back.

CHAPTER 21

ISAIAH

The cacophony of noise swirls around me, the jazz band playing a happy, upbeat tune that's so far removed from how utterly destroyed I feel right now that I can barely process it.

Everyone laughing and drinking around me has no clue what just went down with Athena, that she just ended any hope I had that I might actually have a shot to make things right with her.

I don't know why I thought there could be any other way for this to end, why I bothered to long for more, to hope.

That look in her eyes when she told me to go will haunt me all my days.

"Isaiah?"

My name stops me just outside the door where the main party continues. Artie and Archie made it clear I had to leave, but I can't be rude to someone who recognizes me. That could reflect negatively on Frost Security and do permanent damage to the reputation we've worked so hard for.

I take a breath, plaster a smile on my face, swipe away the tears, and turn back to face whoever called out to me.

Athena's grandmother stands with her shoulders back, a frown tilting her lips down. This woman is on a mission, and it appears to involve me, though I have no idea why. "Where are you going, young man?"

Shit.

I don't have the emotional energy to handle Ruby Warren's inquisition right now. The old woman seems to be the most ready to jump to Athena's defense on family issues, so I can only imagine how angry she must be with me over the revelations from Thanksgiving.

"Mrs. Warren…" I keep that forced smile as long as I can. "Lovely to see you again, but I need to be heading out."

I need to go lick my wounds and drown myself in a bottle of scotch back at the hotel before I fly back to Boston tomorrow.

"Like hell you are." She storms toward me where I stand with my mouth hanging open and grabs my arm, pulling me off to the side of the hallway where we'll be out of view from any of the other Warrens. "I didn't invite you so you could run out of here with your tail tucked between your legs."

What?

"You were the one who sent me the invitation?"

She props her hands on her hips, a look of incredulity crossing her wizened face. "Of course, I was. I knew you would be too thick-headed to come on your own, so I gave you a little nudge."

I release a heavy sigh and run a hand through my hair. "A lot of good it did…"

"I saw you talking to Athena. What happened before my grandsons threw you out?"

"Nothing that hasn't been happening since Thanksgiving.

She's still mad and doesn't want to hear my explanation or apology."

Ruby's eyebrows raise up to her hairline. "You just gave up? You had a challenge, a blip in the road, and you just turn tail and run?"

I open my mouth to answer, then close it because there isn't any reason to argue with this sweet old woman. "I'm leaving to keep from hurting her. I'm leaving to make it easier for her to move on, not because she isn't worth fighting for."

My God, I'd fight to the death for Athena if I thought there was one piece of her that could still care for me.

As her lined face softens, Ruby reaches out and rests a wrinkled hand on my arm. "You love her."

"Of course, I do. I've been a total wreck since Thanksgiving. I've barely slept. Barely worked. I'm a walking shadow of myself because she won't return my calls and I can't live with knowing how I've hurt her."

I had hung all my hopes on her forgiving me tonight, or at least on her opening the door for us to maybe at least *talk* about what happened and work our way toward her forgiving me.

But she shot me down so hard, I can still feel her words slamming into me like bullets.

The tiny hand on my arm squeezes gently. "I appreciate you loving her enough to give her some space. But I wish you would stay and give her a chance to come to her senses before you go back to Boston." She sighs softly and glances back toward the party. "She misses you. She's been a mess since Thanksgiving."

Not what I wanted to hear.

I know how badly the truth hurt Athena, but her grandmother's words at least prove the woman I love, at one time,

209

felt the same way about me. Though, that only seems to twist the knife in my gut more.

Get out of here.

The breakdown I'm about to have can't happen in front of all these people who know Dad and the company. I have to get out of this building and away from the woman who smashed my heart before I collapse into a withering mess of tears and try to destroy something in my anger.

I force another smile. "Thank you for your invitation, Mrs. Warren, and your words of encouragement. But I need to go before your grandsons come running with shotguns."

She barks out a laugh. "Oh, those two don't hunt, thankfully, but the security for tonight is packing heat, so I hear."

The fact that they didn't hire Frost Security for this event should annoy me, but since we never had the contract in previous years, I guess it's not because of bad feelings toward the family. Thankfully.

I lean down and press a kiss to Ruby's cheek, then hustle down the hall and toward the rear exit, trying to put as much distance between the Warrens and me as possible.

The exit sign looms above me, and I race toward it, the bow tie at my neck suddenly tightening like a noose, making it hard for me to draw in a breath. I tug at it wildly and barrel toward the rear entrance, practically ripping it off the hinges as I crash into it, forcing it open.

Thankfully, no other partygoers are congregating outside.

People can't see me like this.

Not with the tears streaming down my face.

Not when I'm crumbling...

ATHENA

Isaiah disappears out the door, taking my heart with him, and I press my hand over my mouth to keep myself from sobbing and making an even bigger scene than we already have.

Artie turns back to me, the small, wrapped gift Isaiah came with in his hands. "Do you want this? I can get rid of it…"

"No." I shake my head. "I mean, yes, I want it."

He raises an eyebrow at me and glances at Archie. "You sure?"

I nod and hold out a hand to accept the gift. Reluctantly, he hands it to me, but I can't bring myself to open it. Not now. Maybe not ever.

Not when I just let Isaiah walk away when all I wanted was to have him pull me into his arms and hold me again.

"Did I make a mistake?"

Artie rests a hand on my shoulder and squeezes. "Not if you're not ready to talk to him or forgive him." He glances around the party at Mother and Father and Grandfather, Penelope, Max, and Blaire, and sighs. "But you should forgive him eventually, even if you two can't be together because of what happened. Holding grudges will only destroy you inside, Athena. And having regrets will do worse."

Oh, God.

I *did* make a mistake. Isaiah has tried to talk to me, tried to explain, called and called, and he came all the way here so I couldn't ignore him, and I wouldn't even hear him out.

The Warrens have all lived with regrets, and I don't want to. I'm too young to wonder for the rest of my life if I made a bad call.

"Athena?" Archie wraps an arm around me. "Are you okay?"

I look up at him and shake my head. "No, I have to go."

"Go? Go where?"

Pulling out of his hold, I offer him and Artie an apologetic half-smile. "To find out what's in this damn box."

Neither of them tries to stop me as I race down the stairs and across the dance floor toward the door. Grandmother offers me a little half-wave from where she stands just inside it, almost as if she's been waiting for me there.

These damn heels pinch my feet and slow my progress, but I finally see the door and push into it. It flies open under my pressure, and I stumble and almost end up face-first on the pavement of the alley behind the museum.

"Shit. Damn."

"You kiss your mother with that mouth, Princess?"

I freeze, closing my eyes against the fresh tears that rise, stinging the backs of my eyes just from the sound of his voice and sexy laugh that sounds so out of place after the way we just left things inside a few moments ago.

Everything I want to say rolls around on the tip of my tongue, but I came out here to get answers.

"Princess?" His lips caress my nickname, and I have to fight the urge to run straight to him and throw myself into his arms.

But I need to know where he stands, where *we* stand.

It's been too long without him.

A month without his touch, his embrace, his lips on mine. Four painful weeks without the comfort and safety I once felt with him. My cheeks heat at the memory of the things he did to me, and my heart beats a rapid tattoo, my breath rushing out in small pants.

Get your shit together, Athena.

"Did this"—I motion between us—"did *I* ever mean anything to you? Was any of this real to you?"

My voice betrays my emotions as my stomach churns in

knots, waiting for his answer. He's apologized over and over again, even said the words I wanted to hear so badly, but I couldn't trust them then. I don't even know if I can trust them now, but I want to hear it all the same.

Isaiah stares at me, mouth agape, pain etched on his handsome, smooth face. "Of course. My God, Athena. You mean *everything* to me."

He scrapes his hand down his face while I just stare at him in stunned silence.

Does he mean that? Did he mean it when he said those three other words?

I want to believe him. He showed up tonight. He knew he was walking into the lion's den with angry, hungry, rabid animals and did it anyway. That has to mean *something*.

What do you have to lose?

It's the question Grandmother asked me the last time we spoke about Isaiah, when I was still staring at voicemails I refused to listen to, and as I stand here, looking at the man who holds my heart, my very future in his hands, I can honestly answer...*everything*.

I flex my fingers around the gift he brought for me and raise the box slowly.

"Open it." His words come harsh and unsteady, like he has to fight to get them out.

My hands shake as I follow his order and slowly remove the wrapping paper and lift the lid off the box.

Oh, my God...

Even in the dim lighting out here in the alley, the beautiful petrified wood jewelry dish that I wanted to buy for myself when we were in Arizona almost shines.

I reach in and pull it out, letting the box fall to the pavement. "How?"

His gaze softens, and he takes a step toward me. "I saw how you looked at it in that souvenir shop and wanted to be sure that whenever you look at it, you thought of your jour-ney, *our* journey, and would always have a small token of that time together. So, I bought it that day and tucked it away in our gear before you came back to the bike."

God, this man.

I want to run to him and throw myself into his arms. Tell him all of the things that were on my mind Thanksgiving night that were left unsaid, but the back door flies open again, and two men in suits with earpieces step out and dart their gazes from me to Isaiah.

"Ms. Warren, is everything okay out here?" The bigger of the two security guards offers Isaiah a suspicious look.

Crap.

"Yes, we're fine. Thank you."

The two men wait another moment before closing the door, but I'm sure they're standing just inside it, should I need them.

Isaiah motions to the door. "If they were my men, they wouldn't have left you out here, no matter what you said."

For some reason, Isaiah "correcting" our security team makes laughter bubble up my throat. His lips curl into a smile before he joins me, his laugh echoing down the alley.

He takes a slow step toward me, then another, until he's close enough to reach out and brush the hair back from my face. "Missed you, Princess."

I sigh and lean into his palm at my cheek, but I can't let the warmth and familiarity distract me from what needs to happen. "Bikes..."

"What, Princess?"

"You know you can't treat me like a child who can't take care of herself and who can't handle the truth, right?"

He winces. "I know. And I am so sorry I didn't just tell you the truth from the moment you stopped at my table."

"I never would have sat down if you had."

A grin plays on his lips. "True. And if I had told you, would you have still asked me to drive you back here? Or would you have just resigned yourself to hopping onto the family jet?"

It's something I've asked myself a hundred or maybe a thousand times since Thanksgiving.

What would I have done?

"I probably would have flown commercial just to piss off my mom."

Isaiah barks out a laugh. "So, your ass would have been sore from the cross-country flight in those tiny seats instead of from being on my bike."

"Probably." I drop my forehead against his chest and inhale that leathery scent that's all Bikes. "But then this"—I motion between us—"never would have happened. There would have never been a Princess and Bikes."

He shakes his head. "No, there wouldn't have been. But there also wouldn't be this massive lie I told, causing this wedge between us."

I drag my head back and sigh, staring into the same green eyes I did that first night when I thought he was Prez272. "It's only keeping us apart if we let it, right?"

His entire body goes rigid, and he tilts my face up even higher. "Do you mean that, Princess? Can you really forgive me for what I did?"

Another question I haven't been able to stop pondering for a month. But this one is a far easier answer than I imagined it would be when the time to say it finally came.

"Yes, I can. I love you, Bikes."

"Christ, Athena, I love you, too."

His lips descend on mine quickly, stealing anything else I might say with a kiss designed to stake his final claim on something he's owned the entire time—my heart that has somehow started beating normally again now that I'm in his arms.

Isaiah may not have turned out to be the man I thought he was, but Bikes is, and when it comes right down to it, Isaiah *is* Bikes, whether he's dressed in old leather with a week's worth of beard on his face or in a five-thousand-dollar tuxedo.

And the fact that he's the perfect Warren husband, the type of partner the family always tried to push me toward, is just one minor flaw in a man who is otherwise perfect for me.

Something tells me that this is going to be the end of fake dates for me and the beginning of a new era for the Warren family holidays, one in which no one tries to control our futures or choose who or what is best for us anymore. One where the only thing we bicker about at the table is who gets the last slice of pie.

ISAIAH

"I cannot wait to get you out of that dress." I whisper the words in Athena's ear, adding a little nip to her diamond-studded lobe to further emphasize my point.

Her grip on my thigh underneath the table intensifies, and her usually pale cheeks turn a beautiful shade of pink.

"Isaiah, stop it." She cautiously scans the dining room at her parents' house to make sure no one suspects what might be happening in our little zone of the table. "We have an entire Christmas dinner with my family to get through first."

And it would be so much easier if she weren't wearing a dress that exposes the swell of her beautiful breasts and hugs every single one of her curves like it was painted on her.

She laughs and playfully swats my arm, but before she can pull away fully, I grab her hand and plant a kiss to the back, letting my lips linger against her smooth skin for just a moment longer than is probably appropriate at any family dinner table, let alone at the Warrens.

My eyes catch on the brilliant diamond that shines on her ring finger—the symbol of a promise yet to be fulfilled.

"I can't wait to marry you."

Archie and Blaire filter into the enormous dining room to take their seats, interrupting my whispered words to Athena.

Archie protectively guards the newest member of the Warren clan in his arms. I barely got Avaleigh out of his grip in the study earlier to give a bit of love to their little addition. But even that tiny bundle of theirs can't derail my thoughts for very long.

I lean toward Athena again, wrapping my arm around the back of her chair. "What if we just run away right now? We'll elope—just you and me and a justice of the peace somewhere. Take off on the bike like old times."

Just like when I proposed to her. Our ride from the southernmost point in Florida to Seattle so we could cross the country together the other direction couldn't have gone better. Lots of laughter. Lots of interesting roadside attractions. Lots of sex in Drakeston Hotels since they're now one of Frost Security's largest clients. And as we watched the sun set from the boat on the Puget Sound, I somehow managed to convince this beautiful woman to be my wife.

But before she can respond to my elopement suggestion, the doorbell sounds and a familiar voice pierces the air. "Hey, we made it!"

I look away from my bride-to-be, and Artie, Penelope, Max, and Persephone come into view.

Athena pulls her hand from mine and pushes to her feet. "I thought you couldn't get here in time for dinner?"

I stand to shake Artie's hand while Athena hugs her sister-in-law and nephew and coos over her niece.

Artie claps me on the back and offers me a wide grin. "The traffic cleared up faster than we expected, thankfully.

It's always hard to know what it will be like driving into the city on Christmas."

"Well, I'm glad you guys are here."

"How are you doing? How's business?"

Though I've grown closer with Artemis and Archimedes since Athena and I "officially" got together, with Artie in Cape Harmony and Artie here in New York and Athena and me in Boston, we don't always have a lot of time to catch up.

"It's going well. Thanks for asking. Frost Security is doing great things in the hospitality sector. Landing that Drakeston contract really boosted that side of the business."

James and Jacob have taken that contract they secured while I was winning Athena's heart and managed to expand it to encompass more hotels and a few sports arenas. And their increased involvement means less workload for me, which means I get to spend more time with my lady and our bike.

"That's good. You need to schedule a meeting with Archie. The contract for Warren Enterprises should be up soon, if memory serves me correctly." Artie looks to Archie for confirmation.

Archie nods. "Yes, I think it is up at the end of January. You definitely should call my sexy secretary and set up a meeting."

He waggles his eyebrows and laughs.

"Archie!" Blaire squeals, punching Archie in the arm while we all join his laughter.

"What?" He feigns innocence. "But seriously, call us. We'll schedule a meeting."

"I'll call. Thanks, guys."

Landing the contract for all of the Warren businesses and events they host would be a major coup—and a happy side effect of marrying into the family. I will see everyone back in

Boston at New Year's and can fill them in on the potential good news.

Bunny Warren appears in the hallway outside the dining room with her perfectly shaped eyebrows raised at the raucous laughter emanating from the room that usually holds a much more somber tone, her husband in tow. "Artie, Penelope, you all made it!"

"They did?" Athena's grandmother's voice carries in from farther down the hall before Ruby and Artemis, the first, appear next to Bunny.

"Grandma! Grandpa!" Max charges toward his grandmother while Persephone chatters and squirms to get loose from Penelope's grip.

Bunny scoops up Persephone and wraps the other arm around Max, kissing the top of his head. "Penelope, you and my son make beautiful babies."

She peppers Persephone's cheek with kisses, which makes the baby giggle while everyone watches.

Penelope offers Bunny a genuine smile, something that wouldn't have been possible only a short time ago. "That's so sweet. Thank you, Bunny."

Bunny scans the room while everyone hugs and kisses one another before settling into their seats. "Are we all ready for dinner?

Athena kisses her mother on the cheek as she takes Persephone away from her.

I can't stop the smile from spreading across my face watching the Warrens interact so easily and with so much true love between them. It's an entirely different dynamic than what I walked into a year ago. This family has grown and changed in so many different ways—and for the better. Which has made Athena far happier than she was on that Thanksgiving day—though I would like to hope I had a role in that, too.

Athena's grandfather settles into his seat at the foot of the table to my left and leans toward me. "Isaiah. You ready to marry my granddaughter?"

"I have been since the day I met her, sir."

The words come easily because they're true. I may not have realized it at the time, but it was a higher power that brought me to Whiskey Jack's that night to intervene in Athena's fate. Something or someone knew I not only needed a break from the hustle and bustle of my life but that what I really needed was *her*.

I look over to Athena sitting with her niece in her lap beside me and can't help but think of the day when we will be a married couple at this very table with children of our own. She grins up at me, her blue eyes sparkling, and to see her so serene and regal makes my heart skip a beat.

I'll never regret stepping in to give this amazing woman a ride across the country.

At that time, I thought I was doing her some sort of favor, but really, she was the one who saved me. Athena helped me realize that there's more to life than what I was doing and having her by my side makes it truly worth living.

ATHENA

The holidays have always been a source of tension and misery in the Warren household for as far back as I can remember, but tonight, it kind of feels like a Christmas miracle has happened because this was almost…relaxing.

Things have been insanely hectic as I juggle planning a wedding and law school while still trying to get my bearings in a new city as big as Boston, but being here with everyone without bickering or ultimatums being thrown around is a whole new world for the Warrens. One that warms my heart and makes my decision to agree to work at Warren Enterprises Worldwide after I graduate really feel like the right one.

Grandfather and Father always imagined all three of the Warren kids running the company together, and only a year or two ago, we never could have seen it becoming a reality.

But what they almost lost taught them to appreciate what they had, and the agreement to let Artie continue his private practice from North Carolina while handling the company's legal issues from there until I can graduate and get my bearings seemed to pacify the old men looking to establish their legacy. And something tells me when the time comes for Artie to step back and for me to take the reins, he won't be so willing to let it go again as he was a few years ago.

If Grandfather and Father do manage to keep all three of us working for them indefinitely, they'll have everything they've ever wanted for the business, and we will all have what we want for ourselves personally.

I push my empty plate away and pat my full stomach. "Dinner was excellent, Mother."

She dabs the corner of her mouth with her cloth napkin. "Thank you, Athena, darling. Speaking of dinner, have you decided who you want to cater your wedding or what you may want to serve? I have several ideas, actually."

Of course, she does.

Our wedding may not be until this summer, but Bunny Warren has been gung-ho about planning every minute detail as soon as humanly possible. Things with the Warrens may be different than they were a year ago, but one thing will never change—Bunny Warren loves to plan and throw a party.

Isaiah cuts me a knowing look and a little half-grin, then reaches under the table to squeeze my thigh, offering me support, solidarity, and a reminder to use kid gloves with Mother so I don't ruin what has been a lovely family dinner.

I force a smile. "Mother, we haven't decided anything yet. If we need some advice, we know where to find you.

Father pats her hand and winks at me, amusement turning the corner of his mouth up, and I catch Grandmother covering her laugh with her hand.

"Oh, yes." Mother flits a hand dismissively. "Of course. Only some thoughts. Who wants pie?"

On cue, the servers enter the dining room again and place plates of chocolate pie in front of everyone around the table.

Every now and again, we still need to reel Mother in or she'll take over. It's just how she was built, but it's a side of her I have learned to handle in a way that won't start Warren War III.

I scan the table while we eat our Christmas dessert, and it is hard to believe the love and laughter pouring from this enormous house that holds almost all of the people I love.

Avaleigh coos in Blaire's arms to my right, and I reach over and snatch her up to give her mom a break and also because I can't pass up baby snuggles. She settles against my chest and tugs playfully on my hair. Isaiah grins at me and winks, and a warmth spreads through my body that can only be one thing—absolute joy.

It's still hard to get used to sometimes. We aren't the same family we used to be—and that's definitely something to celebrate. And having a man like Isaiah love me and care for me and tolerate my crazy family only makes things even better.

Not that the Frosts don't have their own idiosyncrasies and issues, too, but knowing that Isaiah is willing to accept the Warrens and me with all of our issues feels like winning the damn lottery.

Avaleigh coos again and flails in my arms, and I let her grab onto my finger and pull it into her mouth.

"You need to have one or two of those." Artie feeds Persephone a bite of pie. "After Isaiah marries you, that is."

Good save, bro.

I stare down at the little bundle and consider my not-so-distant future.

Isaiah is ready to have kids, and he'll be a great father. I can tell just from the way he treats my nieces and nephew. He loves them just as much as I do. But he'll never push me. He understands I'm behind him significantly when it comes to life and career. He also knows just how badly I want to finish law school and get a few years of work in before our world gets turned upside down by little ones. He'll wait until I'm ready, and the longer I stare at Avaleigh, the harder it is to imagine putting off having Isaiah's child for potentially years. So, it may be coming sooner rather than later.

He reaches over and takes Avaleigh from me, gathering her protectively into his arms like she's the most precious thing he's ever held. I grin at him as he settles her onto his lap then starts eating his pie.

A year ago, this man stole me away from my planned future in Berkeley, and we went on an epic adventure across this great country. What I didn't know at the time was that, in fact, he was stealing my heart.

He's brought so many wonderful things into my life, and because of him and our adventure, all the Warrens are closer than we have been in ages.

I kiss his cheek and whisper into his ear, "I love you, Bikes."

He gives me that same grin he did the first time I saw him on that damn motorcycle. "I love you, too, Princess."

Sitting here, surrounded by everyone I love the most, with my future laid out before me, full of hope and all the amazing things I know are coming, it's clear I truly am the richest woman in the world. This amazing, quirky family is mine—for better and for worse.

"Who wants this last piece of pie?"

We hope you enjoyed *Holiday Fake Date,* the final book in the Warren Family Holidays Series.

If you haven't already read Artemis' and Archimedes' stories, they're available now!

Holiday Terminal: www.books2read.com/HolidayTerminal

Holiday Bridal Wave: www. books2read.com/HolidayBridalWave

Stay up to date on all news, sales, and releases by joining Gwyn's newsletter list here: www. gwynmcnamee.com/newsletter

ABOUT THE AUTHOR - GWYN MCNAMEE

Gwyn McNamee is an attorney, writer, wife, and mother (to one human baby and two fur babies). Originally from the Midwest, Gwyn relocated to her husband's home town of Las Vegas in 2015 and is enjoying her respite from the cold and snow. Gwyn has been writing down her crazy stories and ideas for years and finally decided to share them with the world. She loves to write stories with a bit of suspense and action mingled with romance and heat.

When she isn't either writing or voraciously devouring any books she can get her hands on, Gwyn is busy adding to her tattoo collection, golfing, and stirring up trouble with her perfect mix of sweetness and sarcasm (usually while wearing heels).

Gwyn loves to hear from her readers.
Here is where you can find her:
Facebook:
https://www.facebook.com/AuthorGwynMcNamee/
Twitter:
https://twitter.com/GwynMcNamee
Instagram:
https://www.instagram.com/gwynmcnamee
Bookbub:
https://www.bookbub.com/authors/gwyn-mcnamee
FB Reader Group:
https://www.facebook.com/groups/1667380963540655/

Website:
https://www.gwynmcnamee.com

WAR

Out on the water, I'm in control.

I don't make mistakes.

But the fiery redhead destroyed my plans and

left me no choice.

I had to take her.

Now I'm fighting for my life while battling my growing attraction for my hostage.

Grace may have started my downfall, but she could also be my salvation.

GRACE

The moment he stepped foot on my ship, I knew he was trouble.

He took me, and now, my life is in his hands.

But things aren't what they seem, and Warwick isn't

who he appears.

The man who holds me hostage is slowly working his way into my heart even as greater dangers loom on the horizon.

War and Grace.

Dark and light.

Love and hate.

This storm may destroy them both...

AVAILABLE NOW AT ALL RETAILERS:

books2read.com/SquallLine

Rogue Wave (Book Two)

CUTTER

Complete the mission.

It's what I was trained to do—no matter what.

But when things go to shit right in front of me, my objective gets compromised by a set of fathomless amber eyes.

This isn't a woman's world.

Yet, Valentina refuses to see how dangerous the course she's plotted really is.

How dangerous I am.

VALENTINA

The man who saved my life is just as lethal as the one trying to take it.

Maybe even more.

While he may have rescued me, in the end,

Cutter is my enemy.

The one intent on destroying everything I've striven for.

But the scars of his past draw me closer even though I know I should move away.

Cutter and Valentina.

Anger and desire.

Fight and surrender.

This wave may drag them both under…

AVAILABLE AT ALL RETAILERS:

Safe Harbor (Book Three)

PREACHER

When it comes to firewalls, no one gets

through my defenses.

For the past five years, protecting this band of f-ed up brothers has been my mission.

But Everly pulls me from my cave and does the one thing no one else ever has...

She makes me believe there's a life outside the world

on my screens.

Too bad actions have consequences, ones that threaten everything and everyone around me.

Including the beautiful tattoo artist who has managed to etch herself onto my heart.

EVERLY

The emotional upheaval of the last six months would be enough to break anyone.

And I can already feel myself cracking.

A tall, sexy, tattooed bad boy is the last thing I need thrown into the mix.

All I want is to keep my head down and pour my pain

into my art.

But Preacher walks into my life and offers me safety in a world where I thought there was none.

Until our pasts finally catch up with us…

Preacher and Everly.

Fear and loss.

Hope and heartbreak.

This harbor may be their salvation.

AVAILABLE AT ALL RETAILERS:

books2read.com/SafeHarbor

Anchor Point (Book Four)

ELIJAH

Life outside the walls of my prison cell is far harder than the time I did inside.

There, I had my misery to keep me company.

Out here, I'm forced to face the reality of

everything I've lost.

Nothing can repair the gaping hole in my chest.

Yet, a broken woman wrapped in chains threatens to unravel the tangle of excuses I use to keep everyone

at arm's length.

But letting Evangeline into my world means exposing her to the real threat.

Me.

And all the terrible things that come along with that.

EVANGELINE

Taken.

Enslaved.

To be sold to the highest bidder.

The monsters who stole me away from my life

have no conscience.

I'm not so sure the man who rescues me is any different.

He's an ex-con and a pirate— not to be trusted.

But the dark veil of anguish that shrouds him can't hide the truth of who he is at his core.

Elijah isn't the enemy.

He may be broken and tormented...

And exactly what I need.

Elijah and Evangeline.

Agony and regret.

Faith and acceptance.

This anchor may pull them both down...

AVAILABLE AT ALL RETAILERS:

books2read.com/AnchorPoint

Dark Tide (Book Five)

RION

There is no black and white in this life.

The line between right and wrong blurs.

I'm constantly crossing it.

Saving a life is just as easy as taking one.

And I'm damn good at both.

Finding a woman who can survive in this world was never on the radar.

But Gabriella pulls me from the bottom of a bottle and touches me in a way no one else can.

Too bad secrets and lies have a way of catching up with everyone.

GABRIELLA

How did I end up here, slinging drinks at a dive bar in the middle of nowhere?

The choices that brought me to this were never even a glimmer of possibility only a few years ago.

How things can change so fast…

And now, my path puts me on a collision course

with Orion Gates.

His bigger-than-life size and personality should

be a warning.

The profession he's chosen should be the ultimate

final straw.

But instead, I find myself unable to resist his pull.

A decision that could lead to the end of all of us.

Rion and Gabriella.

Lust and lies.

Betrayal and ruin.

This tide may drown everyone…

AVAILABLE AT ALL RETAILERS:

books2read.com/DarkTide

The Hawke Family Series

Savage Collision **(The Hawke Family - Book One)**

He's everything she didn't know she wanted. She's everything he thought he could never have.

The last thing I expect when I walk into The Hawkeye Club is to fall head over heels in lust. It's supposed to be a rescue mission. I have to get my baby sister off the pole, into some clothes, and out of the grasp of the pussy peddler who somehow manipulated her into stripping. But the moment I see Savage Hawke and verbally spar with him, my ability to remain rational flies out the window and my libido takes center stage. I've never wanted a relationship—my time is better spent focusing on taking down the scum running this city —but what I want and what I need are apparently two different things.

Danika Eriksson storms into my office in her high heels and on her high horse. Her holier-than-thou attitude and accusations should offend me, but instead, I can't get her out of my head or my heart. Her incomparable drive, take-no prisoners attitude, and blatant honesty captivate me and hold me prisoner. I should steer clear, but my self-preservation instinct is apparently dead—which is exactly what our relationship will be once she knows everything. It's only a matter of time.

The truth doesn't always set you free. Sometimes, it just royally screws you.

AVAILABLE NOW AT ALL RETAILERS:

books2read.com/SavageCollision

Tortured Skye (The Hawke Family - Book Two)

She's always been off-limits. He's always just out of reach.

Falling in love with Gabe Anderson was as easy as breathing. Fighting my feelings for my brother's best friend was agonizingly hard. I never imagined giving in to my desire for him would cause such a destructive ripple effect. That kiss was my grasp at a lifeline— something, anything to hold me steady in my crumbling life. Now, I have to suffer with the fallout while trying to convince him it's all worth the consequences.

Guilt overwhelms me—over what I've done, the lives I've taken, and more than anything, over my feelings for Skye Hawke. Craving my best friend's little sister is insanely self-destructive. It never should have happened, but since the moment she kissed me, I haven't been able to get her out of my mind. If I take what I want, I risk losing everything. If I don't, I'll lose her and a piece of myself. The raging storm threatening to rain down on the city is nothing compared to the one that will come from my decision.

Love can be torture, but sometimes, love is the only thing that can save you.

AVAILABLE NOW AT ALL RETAILERS:

Books2read.com/Tortured-Skye

Stone Sober (The Hawke Family - Book Three)

She's innocent and sweet. He's dark and depraved.

Stone Hawke is precisely the kind of man women are warned about — handsome, intelligent, arrogant, and intricately entangled with some dangerous people. I should stay away, but he manages to strip my soul bare with just a look and dominates my thoughts. Bad decisions are in my past. My life is (mostly) on track, even if it is no longer the one to medical school. I can't allow myself to cave to the fierce pull and ardent attraction I feel toward the youngest Hawke.

Nora Eriksson is off-limits, and not just because she's my brother's employee and sister-in-law. Despite the fact she's stripping at The Hawkeye Club, she has an innocent and pure heart. Normally, the only thing that appeals to me about innocence is the opportunity to taint it. But not when it comes to Nora. I can't expose her to the filth permeating my life. There are too many things I can't control, things completely out of my hands. She doesn't deserve any of it, but the power she holds over me is stronger than any addiction.

The hardest battles we fight are often with ourselves, but only through defeating our own demons can we find true peace.

AVAILABLE NOW AT ALL RETAILERS:

books2read.com/StoneSober

Building Storm (The Hawke Family - Book Four)

She hasn't been living. He's looking for a way to forget it all.

My life went up in flames. All I'm left with is my daughter and ashes. The simple act of breathing is so excruciating, there are days I wish I could stop altogether. So I have no business being at the party, and I definitely shouldn't be in the arms of the handsome stranger. When his lips meet mine, he breathes life into me for the first time since the day the inferno disintegrated my world. But loving again isn't in the cards, and there are even greater dangers to face than trying to keep Landon McCabe out of my heart.

Running is my only option. I have to get away from Chicago and the betrayal that shattered my world. I need a new life-one without attachments. The vibrancy of New Orleans convinces me it's possible to start over. Yet in all the excitement of a new city, it's Storm Hawke's dark, sad beauty that draws me in. She isn't looking for love, and we both need a hot, sweaty release without feelings getting involved. But even the best laid plans fail, and life can leave you burned.

Love can build, and love can destroy. But in the end, love is what raises you from the ashes.

AVAILABLE AT ALL RETAILERS:

books2read.com/BuildingStorm

Tainted Saint (The Hawke Family - Book Five)

He's searching for absolution. She wants her happily ever after.

Solomon Clarke goes by Saint, though he's anything but. After lusting for him from afar, the masquerade party affords me the anonymity to pursue that attraction without worrying about the fall-out of hooking-up with the bouncer from the Hawkeye Club. From the second he lays his eyes and hands on me, I'm helpless to resist him. Even burying myself in a dangerous investigation can't erase the memory of our combustible connection and one night together. The only problem… he has no idea who I am.

Caroline Brooks thinks I don't see her watching me, the way her eyes rake over me with appreciation. But I've noticed, and the party is the perfect opportunity to unleash the desire I've kept reined in for so damn long. It also sets off a series of events no one sees coming. Events that leave those I love hurting because of my failures. While the guilt eats away at my soul, Caroline continues to weigh on my heart. That woman may be the death of me, but oh, what a way to go.

Life isn't always clean, and sometimes, it takes a saint to do the dirty work.

AVAILABLE AT ALL RETAILERS:

books2read.com/TaintedSaint

Steele Resolve (The Hawke Family - Book Six)

For one man, power is king. For the other, loyalty reigns.

Mob boss Luca "Steele" Abello isn't just dangerous—he's lethal. A master manipulator, liar, and user, no one should trust a word that comes out of his mouth. Yet, I can't get him out of my head. The time we spent together before I knew his true identity is seared into my brain. His touch. His voice. They haunt my every waking hour and occupy my dreams. So does my guilt. I'm literally sleeping with the enemy and betraying the only family I've ever had. When I come clean, it will be the end of me.

Byron Harris is a distraction I can't afford. I never should have let it go beyond that first night, but I couldn't stay away. Even when I learned who he was, when the *only* option was to end things, I kept going back, risking his life and mine to continue our indiscretion. The truth of what I am could get us both killed, but being with the man who's such an integral part of the Hawke family is even more terrifying. The only people I've ever cared about are on opposing sides, and I'm the rift that could end their friendship forever.

Love is a battlefield isn't just a saying. For some, it's a reality.

AVAILABLE AT ALL RETAILERS:

books2read.com/SteeleResolve

The Slip Series (Romantic Comedy)

Dickslip (A Scandalous Slip Story #1)

One wardrobe malfunction. Two lives forever changed.

Playing in a star-studded charity basketball game should be fun, and it is, until I literally go balls out to show up my arch nemesis. When I dive for the basketball and my junk slips out of my gym shorts, I know my life and career are over. There's no way the network can keep my kids' show on the air after I've exposed myself to millions of people. I don't know how Andy, the new CEO, can go to bat for me with such passion. I also never anticipate how hot she looks in a pair of high heels.

Rafe's dickslip has made my new job even more stressful. It's hard enough being a woman in a man's world without dealing with sex organs being publicly displayed when someone is representing the company. But he's an asset to the network, not to mention hot as hell. I can barely keep my eyes off him or his crotch during our meetings. Defending him to the board puts my ass on the line as much as his, but it's worth it. So is risking my job to fulfill the fantasies I've had about him since he first set foot in my office.

Things may have started out bad, but... some accidents have happy endings.

Nipslip (A Scandalous Slip Story #2)

One nipple. A world of problems.

I own the runway. Until my nipple pops out of my dress during New York Fashion Week and it suddenly owns me. Being called a worthless gutter slut by a fuming designer is the least of my problems. My career is swirling around the toilet like the other models' lunches. Until smoking hot Tate Decker steps in with a crazy idea about how his magazine can maybe salvage my livelihood.

It's less than two feet in front of me. Perfect and perky and pink. And the woman it's attached to looks absolutely horrified. I need to help her, and not just because she's beautiful and has a perfect rack. Using my position in the industry to expose the volatile nature of our business puts my career in jeopardy in an attempt to save Riley's. I'm willing to risk that, but falling for her isn't part of the plan.

When love and tits are involved... Things can get slippery.

Beaver Blunder (A Scandalous Slip Story #3)

One brief mistake. A world of hurt.

No panties. No problem. At least until I slip on the wet floor and go heels over head in front of my colleagues and half the courthouse. Returning to consciousness can't be more awkward, until I find out who my sexy, argumentative, and bossy knight in shining armor really is. My career may not survive my beaver blunder, and my heart might not survive Owen Grant.

Madeline Ryan tumbles into my life on a wave of perfume and public embarrassment. She falls and exposes herself in front of me, and I find myself falling for her despite the fact she fights me every chance she gets. Being a woman in a good ol' boy profession demands a certain brashness, but it definitely has me thinking, maybe litigators shouldn't be lovers.

With stressful jobs and big attitudes, going commando has never been so freeing.

AVAILABLE NOW AT ALL RETAILERS:

www.Books2read.com/BeaverBlunder

ABOUT THE AUTHOR - CHRISTY ANDERSON

Writing with a whole lot of sarcasm and humor, mixed with a bit of Southern charm, Christy Anderson ain't no sweet tea kinda storyteller.

As an author of romance, Christy believes it doesn't always have to be hearts and flowers; sometimes, it is dark and twisted, but romance nonetheless. She mixes terror, revenge, and a sliver of love and hope into stories about family, friends, struggles, blurred lines, and happily-ever-afters.

Christy lives in the beautiful mountains of Eastern Tennessee with her husband and 152 cats (not really, but close), where she enjoys writing one twist at a time.

Web Page (under construction): https://www.christyandersonauthor.com
Facebook: www.facebook.com/Christy-Anderson-Author
Facebook Reader Group: https://www.facebook.com/groups/461018120762644
Goodreads: www.goodreads.com/christy_anderson
Instagram: Christy_Anderson_Author

The Killing Hours

(Dark Romance/Romantic Suspense)

The Hunted (Book One)

My heart beats furiously in my chest trying to keep up with the pace
I have set.

I am running as fast as I can but it is pointless.

They will catch me.

I am only delaying the inevitable, postponing my

fate if you will.

I know what will happen when they catch me.

It's the same ending every time.

Still, I push my legs as fast as they will go, my body aches from the
exertion.

I can hear them behind me.

They are closing in.

This is part of a twisted game.

The goal, to catch their Prey.

Me.

I am the prize for the Hunter.

I am the Hunted.

AVAILABLE NOW: books2read.com/TheHuntedCA

❄

Book Club Novellas

(Romantic Comedy)

Glory Hole (Book One)

Typically, I'm not the kind of girl to spy on someone.

Really. I'm not.

So why, you ask, do I have my eye pressed to the wall of my living room,

spying on him through my own private glory hole?

Have you seen Beckett Jameson?

AVAILABLE NOW: books2read.com/GloryHole

Rim Job (Book Two)

You would think going to Las Vegas to celebrate your best friend's wedding would be a great time.

You'd be wrong.I'm the kind of girl who plays by the rules.

Las Vegas is the place where rules go to die.

I have a checklist for my life, an order in which the things on that list are supposed to happen.

So far, all has gone according to plan.

That is, until one fateful night when I meet him.

My list wasn't prepared for him.

Frankly, neither was I.

What happens in Vegas doesn't always stay there.

AVAILABLE NOW: books2read.com/RimJob

1

Made in the USA
Columbia, SC
29 November 2021

50010428R00143